Dawn's New Day

By the Author

A Reunion to Remember

Dawn's New Day

Dawn's New Day

by

TJ Thomas

2017

DAWN'S NEW DAY

ISBN 13: 978-1-63555-072-6

This Trade Paperback Original Is Published By
Bold Strokes Books, Inc.
P.O. Box 249
Valley Falls, NY 12185

First Edition: October 2017

Credits
Editor: Cindy Cresap
Production Design: Susan Ramundo
Cover Design By Melody Pond

Acknowledgments

To Len Barot, Sandy Lowe, and all the wonderful folks at Bold Strokes Books—thank you for giving us all a place to read and write LGBT fiction. My fellow BSB authors, I continue to learn so much from you and am proud to count you as friends. Thank you to Melody Pond for the beautiful cover.

Domestic violence is a reality in our society that we must speak about to raise awareness and overcome the stigma of victims speaking out about their experiences. If you or someone you know is a victim of domestic violence, in the US, please call the National Domestic Violence Hotline at 1-800-799-7233 or TTY 1-800-787-3224 to get the support you deserve. There are no fees, no names, and no judgment. Only help.

Breast cancer is impacting the lives of and killing too many of our sisters, mothers, aunts, wives, daughters, and friends. One in eight women will be diagnosed with breast cancer in their lifetimes. We need to do more to find a cure. Check out some of the stories on the Breast Cancer Research Foundation website: www.bcrfcure.org.

For my part, a portion of the proceeds from *Dawn's New Day* will be donated directly to the National Domestic Violence Hotline and to the Breast Cancer Research Foundation. I encourage each of you to give to an organization of your choice. Together we can make a difference.

Thank you to my oldest brother, Steve, for always being there even when you lived so far away. Your perseverance through adversity has been an inspiration. Now that I've recognized you in a book you can get over the fact I didn't acknowledge you specifically in the first one. Love you.

The idea for this book began when I still lived in San Diego. However, I made a number of trips back during the writing. Thank you, Diana and Tam, for all the assistance with "research." I especially enjoyed our adventures at Uptown, Snooze, and the Hillcrest Brewing Company.

I am fortunate to have amazing first readers. Your insights, critiques, and questions immensely improved the book. Thank you Aurora, Inger, and Teeps, and to Elle, who once again read every version—I appreciate your constructive critiques and your encouragement every day.

Special thanks to my editor, Cindy Cresap, who uses supportive and humorous feedback to improve my craft of storytelling.

To you, the reader, thank you for making what I love to do mean something.

Most importantly, thanks to my wyf, Elle, for her inspiration, patience, and love. You gave perceptive feedback every time you touched the story, and above all, you believe in me. Our love propels me to be and do better.

Dedication

Elle, I love you more than that.

Chapter One

Dawn Oliver was in her element. She loved creating and tending lush, colorful, fragrant gardens. She enjoyed few things more. Some people thought keeping a garden was work. For her it was pure joy. Spending time in the dirt was one of her deepest pleasures. The smells, the sights, even the feel of her hands in the dirt centered and calmed her.

This was true whether she was in her own yard or at the shelter for abused women where she volunteered twice a week. She taught them basic gardening skills. Sharing the peace that came from working in the garden was deeply gratifying. They had many things to do to rebuild their lives and exist on their own, but time in the garden could be an escape into something almost spiritual. They didn't have to think about bills, job hunting, if they'd be found, or any of the hurdles that lay ahead. Gardening was a respite for Dawn. She was humbled to share that with others.

Dawn heard someone approaching. When she saw the timid, dark-haired woman glance her way, she said, "Good morning, you must be Meg."

"How did you know?"

"When I came in this morning Trish mentioned you were new and that you enjoyed gardening. I haven't seen you around before, so I took a chance. I'm Dawn."

"It's nice to meet you, Dawn. Do you mind if I join you?"

"Of course not. Please do. Do you know where everything is?"

"Yes."

Dawn waited while Meg gathered a few tools and a pair of gloves. Once she was settled a few feet away, Dawn spoke again. "Did you have a garden before you came here?"

Meg slumped her shoulders and frowned. "Yes."

"It's hard to leave something you've nurtured even if you are leaving it to make your life better."

Meg studied Dawn for several moments and then nodded in acknowledgement.

"The great thing about gardening is you can start over, start fresh in a new place. Even with a small patch of dirt, give it care and you can bring things to life. Your garden can blossom anywhere, and it's so much sweeter when you're at peace where your garden is planted."

Meg smiled for the first time. "You have a point."

When she returned home later that morning, Dawn decided to continue working in her own front gardens. Now, with the sun shining on her back and a light breeze against her cheeks, she couldn't be happier. Feeling the soil crumble in her hands and an occasional bee buzzing around—these meant one thing to Dawn: spring, her favorite time of the year. One of the reasons Dawn loved living in San Diego was being out in the yard all year long. Even when the weather wasn't right for growing, she could prune, weed, or work the soil, amending it and preparing it for the coming season.

It was the middle of March, and she was excited spring rains had finally come. She had started her annual adventure a couple of weeks ago. The rains were infrequent anymore. Dawn hummed a catchy tune she heard on the radio earlier while getting ready for her day, not even sure what song it was. She transferred the new flowers from the containers she'd bought when she decided the garden needed more color. Lost in her own world, alone with her plants and flowers, she amused herself with the patterns and lines she wanted to create. In her garden, like on canvas, she often saw the final picture before she brushed the first stroke or planted the first flower.

Occasionally though, she had no idea what would emerge when she started. She knew she would have to return to the studio at some point, but spending time in her gardens each day rejuvenated her and kept her ideas fresh, allowing her painting to flow more freely after she took time outside. It was a careful balance but a necessary one if she was going to make a living as an artist. She knew she was lucky—most artists were never able to support themselves. She did.

A moving truck with a broken muffler pulled into the driveway next door, shattering her solitude. She sat on her heels and watched the new arrivals for a few moments. A sleek motorcycle pulled in beside the truck, and a small SUV pulled up to the curb. From the glimpse she caught of the motorcycle, she knew it was a nice bike. Two large men jumped from the moving truck and moved to the back. She heard the door roll. Then two women climbed out of the SUV, one with collar-length blond hair, the other with wavy brunette hair that flowed past her shoulders. They joined hands and walked toward the house.

Dawn couldn't see the motorcycle or who rode it since the moving truck blocked her view. The quiet mostly returned, with occasional bits of conversation floating across the yard. She returned her attention to her flower bed, enjoying the beautiful day. The rhythm of preparing the soil and transferring plants from pots to ground quickly absorbed her focus. She barely noticed the low hum of activity next door.

❖

After a while, the sun's rays grew too hot and Dawn went inside to cool off. She poured a glass of lemonade and wandered into her studio to ponder her current work in progress. It was coming along nicely. Not quite ready to start painting, she went to the living room and peeked out her front window to see the move progressing next door. As she stood there, she wondered about her new neighbors.

She decided to take over sandwiches and lemonade as a "welcome to the neighborhood" gesture. Surely her new neighbors had their hands full and would be too busy to make lunch. Dawn made a pile of both cold cut and hummus sandwiches. She mixed a fresh batch of lemonade and packed everything in plastic containers and carefully arranged it in a basket. At the last minute, she remembered cups and napkins since the kitchen would not be unpacked yet.

Dawn rang the doorbell and waited. The woman who answered the door was stunning. Dawn had expected one of the women she had seen earlier, and the surprise had her tongue-tied. Standing in the doorway in dark jeans hugging well-toned thighs and a black T-shirt that accentuated firm muscles, was the most gorgeous woman Dawn had ever seen. *Oh my.* Midnight black hair cropped short, gray eyes that darkened as she focused, a strong jaw, and lips that softened the almost too angular face made the whole package one of exquisite beauty. Dawn stood motionless.

She realized she was staring a moment too late. For a moment, Dawn froze. Then the woman glanced at the basket in Dawn's arms, breaking the intense gaze. *Whoa!*

"Hello?"

"Hi, um, I live next door. I thought you all might like some sandwiches and lemonade about now."

"Wow, thanks. Come on in."

"No." Dawn cringed inwardly at the harshness of her tone and softened it. "I mean I don't want to intrude. I just wanted to bring this over." Dawn pushed the basket into the woman's hands and beat a hasty retreat. *Smooth, Dawn, real smooth.*

❖

Dawn stood by the window for a few minutes thinking about the exchange. No woman had ever had such an immediate effect on her. The chiseled features on the olive-skinned, black-haired Adonis were etched in her mind. She shrugged and let it go. It didn't matter. Nothing would happen there. Dawn turned away from the window, walked to her computer, and checked her email.

After she read her sister Ali's latest response about how school and work were going, it was time to stop procrastinating. Dawn changed out of the long-sleeved shirt she wore to protect her fair skin from the sun and into a loose T-shirt already splattered with paint. She strolled into the studio where she spent most of her waking hours.

This was her work, but it was also a pleasure. Nothing came close to the ongoing affair she had with an easel and canvas. Art was always a part of her life. Virtually a constant companion she could count on. Nobody in her life, except her family, had ever been as steady. She thought there was someone that she could count on once, but Lori had turned out not to be that person, and she had been hurt badly. She wasn't going to make that mistake again.

Dawn stepped into the room awash with natural light from the bank of windows on two sides plus the skylights she'd had installed the previous year. Depending on the time of day and the angle of the sun, the shadows cast in the room offered interesting contrasts. The space inspired her creativity. In addition to the easels scattered around the room with paintings, there were blank canvases of various sizes, a drafting table cluttered with sketches, and one entire counter was packed with jars and tubes of paint. It was very full but not cluttered, as Dawn had everything meticulously organized. In the far corner, on a small desk, her work computer contained all the specialized software she needed to create some of her other works of art.

After two years, it still amazed her the way her boutique T-shirt design business had taken off as quickly as it had. The company that bought her original designs back then took over the manufacturing and contracted her to design more. She had added other clients over the last couple of years and made a surprisingly good living, but she would never give up her painting. Like her gardening, it was a part of who she was.

Not so long ago, she had been too hurt and afraid to find the inspiration to paint. She had lost confidence in her skill as an artist because of Lori's insults. It was agonizing. As a result, she now treasured her art more than ever before. Now she nurtured it—art was what pulled her through that dark time. Once she started to turn feelings into colors on a canvas, she let them go. Letting go was creating, but she would never forget.

Dawn picked up her palette and began squeezing the blue, gray, black, and white paints slowly, carefully. The paint emerged from the tubes steadily like caterpillars inching onto the palette. She studied the painting in front of her from several different angles before picking up a brush. From the first stroke of paint across the canvas, she was engrossed. Painting consumed her, freeing her mind of all conscious thought. Her brush moved across the canvas with ease, strokes quickly giving shape to the vision that existed only in her mind. Sometimes she had soft music on in the background. Today, she forgot to turn it on. It didn't matter; it rarely registered anyway.

When she painted, she fell into the colors, the depth, and the textures of her art. Often she lost track of time. She loved the process and those who loved her knew her habits and were never surprised when she didn't answer her phone or even the door. When a sound broke through her concentration, it surprised her.

Dawn set her palette down and laid the brush aside. She stepped away from the painting. Something had distracted her. She heard it again. Someone was knocking on the door. Who could possibly be at her door in the middle of the day? She peeked at her watch. It was later than she thought, much later in fact. She hadn't noticed the hours passing as she was absorbed in her painting. She grabbed a rag to wipe her hands as she made her way to the front door. She glanced out the front window and realized the moving truck was gone. Out of habit, she peered through the peephole and saw the soft butch blonde from the SUV next door. She opened the door. "Hello?"

"Hi, I'm June." She had a contagious and friendly smile that seemed genuine. Dawn couldn't help but return it. "I'm sorry to disturb you. I've been next door helping my friend move in and we want to celebrate with a bottle of wine, but we can't find her wine opener. Would you happen to have one we can borrow?"

"Uh, sure, hang on." As she started to walk away, Dawn remembered her manners. "Actually, why don't you come in out of the heat? It'll only take a minute."

June stepped through the door and closed it behind her. "Thanks, I appreciate it. By the way, thank you for the sandwiches earlier. I had one of each and both were delicious."

"No problem. I'll be right back." Dawn stepped into her studio and swirled her brush through the jar of water next to the easel. Then she went to the kitchen and grabbed her wine opener. She returned to the living room where June was looking at the canvases along one wall.

"Here you go."

June didn't turn from studying the art on the walls. "Is this your work?"

"Yes."

"They're amazing."

"Thank you."

Finally, June turned. "I'm sorry. I didn't even ask your name."

"It's not a prerequisite for borrowing a wine opener."

"So you're not going to tell me?" June asked with amusement.

"I'm Dawn." She held the corkscrew toward June and smiled.

June accepted it but was still examining Dawn's work. "Thanks. Do you ever paint on commission, Dawn?"

"Sure."

"Do you have a card? I would love to have you paint something as a surprise for my fiancée."

Dawn walked to her desk and pulled out one of her business cards. "Here you go. Give me a call when you want to discuss the details."

"Great. I'll do that." June slipped the card into the back pocket of her jeans. "Listen, I should get back. Kate and Cam will wonder if I got lost crossing the yard. That will be funnier when you know me better." She made her way back to the front door, then turned. "Why don't you come over and have a glass of wine with us?"

"Thanks, but I should get back to work."

"On Saturday? Come on, just one glass."

Dawn hesitated. She was leery of spending time with the handsome woman she met earlier, but if there were other people to act as a buffer, she thought it might be the perfect time. "When you work for yourself, there is no such thing as a weekend. But since I do work for myself, I suppose I can take a break and go over for a few minutes. Let me just change my shirt real quick."

"Seriously? We've been moving things for hours. We're sweaty and dusty. If you freshen up you'll make us all realize just how dirty we are."

Dawn examined the paint splattered T-shirt she had pulled on hours earlier. She hesitated. She liked to make the best impression possible and dressed nicely when she left the house, but she didn't want June to feel uncomfortable. She supposed it wasn't all that bad. "Fair enough, but I really do need to wash my brushes first if you wouldn't mind waiting a couple of minutes."

"Sounds like a plan."

Chapter Two

Dawn and June stepped outside, and Dawn pulled the door closed behind them.

"I noticed your flowers on the way over. Your garden is beautiful," June said.

"Thank you."

"Are you this good at everything you do?"

Dawn raised an eyebrow. "I'm not sure I know what you mean."

"Well, you have an award-winning garden in your front yard and incredible works of art hanging on your living room walls. I just wondered if there was anything you don't do well."

"Sure, lots of things."

"Will you tell me one?"

"I can't cook to save my life."

June chuckled. "Thank goodness. We can't have too much perfection in the neighborhood."

Dawn was still shaking her head as she entered the house next door. She saw boxes everywhere but was surprised at the progress. When they walked into the living room, the willowy brunette from the SUV glanced over. She knelt on the floor arranging books from a box on a bookshelf. "Oh, hi. We thought maybe you'd gotten lost."

June glanced at Dawn and rolled her eyes playfully. "Told you." She gave the brunette an easy but affectionate kiss. "Kate, this is Dawn. It is my fault it took so long, but only because I got lost looking at Dawn's paintings. She's quite a talented artist." She turned back to Dawn. "This is my fiancée, Kate."

Dawn extended her hand. "Nice to meet you, Kate."

"You too, Dawn. I'm glad you could join us. I would love to see your work some time."

"Sure, any time."

"I hope June thanked you for lunch. It was very sweet."

"She did. It really wasn't a big deal."

Before Dawn could say anything else, the gorgeous stranger from earlier entered the room. June broke the silence. "I believe you two have already met."

"Not officially. Dawn, is it? It's a pleasure to meet you. I'm Cam. Thanks for lunch and use of the corkscrew."

Cam held out her hand to Dawn. Dawn returned the gesture. When their hands met, Dawn's breath caught. She hoped she was the only one who heard it. Cam's eyes darkened. She was mesmerized as a corner of Cam's mouth lifted into a grin. Dawn mentally shook herself and pulled her hand away as nonchalantly as she could manage. Her hand was warm with sensations. "No problem. It's nice to meet you too."

June and Kate stood behind Cam, so neither saw her smile deepen. It made Dawn's heart gallop in her chest. When Cam turned to her friends, Dawn took her first full breath since Cam entered the room and managed to pull herself together.

"Shall we move this party outside? At the least the yard isn't a moving zone," Cam said.

They headed for the kitchen. Cam grabbed a bottle of wine off the wine rack, June grabbed plastic cups and paper plates, and Kate grabbed the pizza and napkins. They were so in sync Dawn imagined the three of them had done this many times before. June headed into the backyard. Dawn followed her. Kate and Cam quickly joined them.

Dawn tried to calm her racing heart and clear her muddled brain. Luckily, nobody paid much attention to her as she chastised herself. *It's true, Cam's gorgeous. It doesn't matter. You can't let it matter. You have to calm down. She's your neighbor. Just keep it friendly. You can handle this. You're an adult. Just relax and try to enjoy yourself.*

They ended up on the covered patio. As Cam opened the wine, Kate put pizza on plates and June pulled out cups, then she set out napkins. Dawn surveyed the yard. The grill and patio set were already set up, but there was a heavy bag leaning against one of the posts of the patio cover. Then she turned her attention to the yard. It was as deep and wide as hers with almost no landscaping, just green grass all the way back to the fence. Functional, she supposed, but plain, an empty canvas to fill with color. She would love to get her hands on it. She laughed at herself. Then she noticed the gigantic doghouse in the corner of the yard under the one tree in the back corner of the yard. Just as she was about to comment on it, Kate got her attention. "Dawn, would you like some pizza?"

She started to decline until she realized she hadn't eaten since breakfast and it was nearly four in the afternoon. "Sure. I'd love a slice. Thank you."

She rejoined them at the table. When Cam handed her a glass of wine, she took it easily. "Thank you. So, do you have a dog?"

"Yes, two. Jack is a golden retriever and Mozz is a black lab. The boys are staying with friends today. I wanted to spare them the chaos of the move."

"Mozz? That's an interesting name."

Cam inclined her head. "It's short for Mozzarella. Jack's short for Sonoma Jack. All my dogs seem to end up with cheesy names, pun intended. It's become a tradition. When I got my first puppy at ten, I named him Cheddar. I don't know why my parents let me stick with the name, but I guess they decided since he was my dog I should name him."

"That's great," Dawn said.

"I think my favorite name was Muenster," June said.

Everyone laughed.

"Just how long have you all known each other?" Dawn asked.

"Since college," they answered together.

The three of them shared a look like being this in sync was a common occurrence.

Dawn sipped her wine. "It seems like there's a story there."

"So many stories," June said. "We all met the first day of college. The three of us lived on the same floor. Cam and I were roommates and soccer teammates. Kate lived down the hall. The three of us instantly clicked. We hung out all the time, got really close. It got to the point when someone saw one of us they expected to see the other two."

"And you've been the best of friends all this time?"

"Well, not exactly," June admitted. "Like any friendship, ours has had its ups and downs. But we've always made amends and come back together. We can't seem to stay away from each other for long. These two know more about me than anyone in my life. I don't know what I would ever do without either one of them."

"Likewise," Cam said.

"Me either," Kate said softly.

"Wow. That's great. So, June and Kate, is that when you two got together?"

Kate glanced warmly at June. "No. That happened after college. Back then we were so busy trying to deny our feelings and not wanting to ruin our friendship that we made things pretty bad between the three of us for a while. Cam got caught in the middle of a lot of the crossfire. She's the one who finally helped us see what we couldn't or wouldn't see on our own."

"How did you manage that?" Dawn asked Cam.

"I kissed Kate and told June all about it."

"What? You didn't!"

"It's true and I got punched in the face for it," Cam said.

"I had never hit anyone in my life," June said. "I don't know what came over me. One minute Cam is talking, and the next thing I know I'm hot and angry. Then—bam! I didn't think about it. It wasn't a conscious thought. I reacted. I hit her. I still can't believe I did it. And I've never hit anyone since. I didn't know what was going on. Cam did though and she helped me figure it out. I learned a lot about myself that day. Some realizations weren't so good." She turned to Kate. "Others were." June took Kate's hand gently. "Thank the Goddess she did or I would probably still be hiding from the truth."

"Did you know before you kissed Kate that June had feelings for her?" Dawn asked Cam.

"Of course. It was obvious to everyone except the two of them."

"So, why kiss her and risk your friendship? Why not just talk to June about it?"

A mischievous grin spread across Cam's face. "Well, first of all, look at her."

"Why thank you, gorgeous," Kate said.

Cam's smile widened and she met Dawn's intense gaze evenly. "But also I had tried talking to June and I had tried talking to Kate, but both of them were too bullheaded to hear me. So I figured I had to do something to shake things up. Things had gotten pretty bad, and I didn't want to lose either one of them as friends. I figured maybe, just maybe, if each of them could see what she was hiding from, things might get better. There wasn't much chance the situation could get worse. The two of them weren't even speaking to each other by that point. I thought if I could get them riled up enough to at least talk to each other, life might improve for all of us."

"Well, I guess your plan worked."

"It did, eventually," June said. "Kate and I still danced around the issue for a while trying to feel each other out before either one of us would spill our guts. Finally though, I showed up on Kate's doorstep one night and told her we needed to talk."

"So we talked," Kate said.

"And the two of them have been together ever since," Cam said. "I love it when a plan comes together."

Kate stood to refill everyone's wine. "So, Dawn, now that we've talked your ear off, tell us about yourself."

"There's not a lot to tell. I'd rather hear more about ya'll. Besides, it seems the three of you have a lot of stories."

"Ya'll? Are you from the South?" June asked.

"Born and raised in North Carolina. My twang tends to come out when I'm tired or drinking."

"Tell us more about you," June said.

Dawn thought a moment. "Okay, let's see. I have my own business designing T-shirts. I also paint and am currently working on several pieces for a show next month. I love gardening and spend as much time as possible in my yard. What do you all do for work?"

"I'm a computer programmer," June said.

Kate said, "I'm a dance instructor at night, which is my passion, but I'm also a substitute teacher for elementary school."

When everyone looked at her, Cam said, "And I'm an IT Manager for a midsized company in Hillcrest."

Dawn had hoped by asking about their work, they'd forget to come back to her. Not so easily put off, June and Kate started to ask questions over one another. "How long have you lived here?" "Is your family here?" "Any great loves?" "Besides gardening what do you do for fun?"

Dawn laughed at the rapid-fire questions. "What is this, speed dating?"

June and Kate laughed at themselves too. June said, "We're just curious about you."

"Well, thank you. Let's see…I've lived in San Diego for about eleven years, but I only bought my house here in Normal Heights about two years ago. My parents still live in the same town where I grew up in North Carolina, but my little sister, Ali, recently moved to Seattle to work on her doctorate. Besides gardening, I like to go dancing and to classic car shows. Sometimes I think I was born in the wrong decade because I love the fifties styles so much."

"You forgot one," Kate said.

"What's that?"

"Any great loves?"

Dawn looked away before answering softly, "No."

Cam, who had watched the exchange silently up to this point, said, "That surprises me. You're very attractive."

Dawn felt herself blush and silently cursed her pale skin. On impulse, she used the same mockingly seductive tone that Kate had used earlier. "Well, thank you, gorgeous. You're not so bad yourself."

June and Kate laughed heartily. For the time being, the subject was dropped, much to Dawn's relief. It took her a few seconds, but she realized Cam saved her from having to answer. She glanced over and became aware that she was being studied. She held Cam's gaze for a moment and silently mouthed, "Thank you."

Cam inclined her head slightly to acknowledge Dawn and then she turned back to June and Kate. This allowed Dawn time to do some studying of her own.

❖

Cam stood with Dawn at the bottom of the porch. She waved to June and Kate as they climbed into their truck. As June drove off, Dawn turned to Cam. "Well, I'll see you around."

"I'll walk you home."

Dawn stopped. "That's silly. You can see my porch from here."

"Humor me. I don't like to let a lady walk home alone."

"Suit yourself."

Walking beside Dawn for a moment in silence, Cam surveyed the gardens in Dawn's front yard. Even in the waning light, she could see the riot of colors, which at first glance appeared to be random. But when she took a second look, Cam could see it was all a part of a well-planned pattern. "You have a beautiful yard. Did you do all this?"

Genuine pleasure lit Dawn's entire face. "Yes, thanks."

The wall Cam sensed between them all evening came down for a moment. Dawn was even more beautiful when her defenses lowered. She wondered again what had happened to Dawn to make those defenses necessary.

At her front porch, Dawn turned to Cam. "Good night."

"Sweet dreams, Dawn. Thanks again for everything. You've made us feel at home."

Dawn smiled. "Sure thing." She hurried into her house.

❖

Before the sun breached the horizon the next morning, Cam was already hard at work organizing her things. She wanted to have the majority of the boxes unpacked and put away before she picked up the dogs later that day. Dawn's striking face stuck with her. It was beautiful and pale with the faintest dusting of freckles across her cheeks and nose. The afternoon sun had glinted off the deep red hair that was pulled up and away in a haphazard bun. A blush of color had crept across those cheeks when their eyes locked. There had been interest in those green eyes when they first met yesterday afternoon. Cam was sure of it. She hadn't decided how she felt about the fact that her last thoughts before sleep overtook her and her first thoughts this morning swirled around Dawn.

It had been years since that place was held by anyone other than Melanie. From the day she and Mel met, they were in sync. She had been the love of her life. They'd planned to be together forever. Then she'd gotten sick and worse. The devastation in Cam's heart had overwhelmed her for a while, but Mel had helped her see that Cam wasn't the one leaving. She needed to figure out how to continue to have a full life even after Mel was gone.

Cam had reached the conclusion that meant a full life on her own because she never expected to be interested in anyone else. Mel had claimed her heart. Before she'd died, she made Cam promise that she wouldn't ever turn her back on the potential of finding someone else. Mel hadn't wanted her to be alone forever. It was an easy promise to make because she didn't think it would ever be an issue. She couldn't imagine finding a spark like she had with Mel with anyone else.

Cam led a full life. She loved her work. She had wonderful, enriching friendships. She volunteered. There were days she still thought of Melanie and missed her painfully, but she had had time to say good-bye. She tried to make a life for herself Melanie would be proud of, and she was tremendously fulfilled. Recently, she had dated casually, but was happy being on her own. She didn't think she ever wanted a serious relationship again.

For the first time since she'd made that pledge to Mel, that she wouldn't close herself off, she found herself intrigued. She always found women interesting and enticing, but it wasn't often she couldn't figure one out without much difficulty. There had been sparks between her and Dawn when she had taken her hand. Cam had flirted lightly throughout the evening but hadn't received the slightest indication of any type of response.

For the umpteenth time, she reviewed what she knew, although Cam admitted it wasn't much. Dawn was an artist, businesswoman, and gardener. She drank wine, ate pizza, and somewhere in her past, she had been hurt badly. Cam realized she was only guessing about that last piece of information, but she'd seen Dawn's face last night when Kate and June pressed her to answer their questions about her great loves. Cam couldn't get that haunted expression out of her mind. She shook her head trying to clear it. She'd seen and felt Dawn's initial reaction to her, but then Dawn hadn't responded to her the rest of the night in any way other than as a friendly neighbor.

She had two options: forget about it or gather more data. Cam easily admitted she already knew she had to find out more. She couldn't ignore such an intriguing woman right next door. She would have to learn her story. Cam laughed at herself. *Time to get the pups*. At the moment, her doorbell rang. *Right on time.*

Cam opened the door. "Hey, Cindy."

"Hi, sweets."

Cam opened the door wider. "Want to see the place first?"

Cindy stepped into the house. "Yes! I can't believe it took you so long to ask."

Cam gave Cindy a quick tour of the house before heading out.

As the first rays of sun peeked through the window, Dawn woke and stretched her whole body. She'd dreamt about a tall, dark, sexy woman. It didn't take any time at all to picture Cam. She was all of those things and gorgeous. *Cam is too handsome for her own good, and mine too for that matter*. Dawn gave herself a moment to feel everything. Then she shook her head and climbed out of bed. *It doesn't matter how handsome my new neighbor is or how nice she seems. I am not going there. I'm not putting myself in that position ever again.*

She planned on working for a couple of hours before giving herself a break to plant some new annuals in the backyard. But first she needed coffee. As she passed through the living room, she glanced outside and saw a truck at Cam's place. At that moment, she saw Cam and a stunning blonde walk out to the truck arm in arm. They appeared to be engaged in deep, intimate conversation with their heads close together.

Cam opened the passenger side door for the blonde and walked around to climb in the driver's side. Cam pulled down the driveway, and Dawn quickly lost sight of the vehicle as it rounded a curve in the road. *Well, that makes things easier*. Given this new information it should have been a piece of cake to put Cam out of her mind. She had a girlfriend. Therefore she was completely off limits. Even if Dawn dated, she wouldn't ever date someone who was with someone else. So why couldn't she forget about Cam? Dawn went back to the kitchen. She still needed coffee.

Chapter Three

The following weekend, Dawn was busy at her studio computer when the doorbell rang. She had spent the better part of the day working on a new T-shirt design. She wasn't expecting anyone, but since Cam moved in next door, either June or Kate popped over occasionally to see if she wanted to join them. It hadn't escaped her notice Cam was never the one who invited her over. She always had fun, especially with Kate and June, but she remained cautious around Cam.

Dawn peeked through the peephole to see who was at the door. She smiled as she opened the door to Kate. "Well, hi there."

"Hi, yourself."

"Come in. What are you up to?"

"We're hanging out at Cam's. She's about to grill steaks, and we're talking about going bowling afterward. We wondered if you'd be interested in joining us for either or both?"

An image of the blonde she saw with Cam the other day floated through Dawn's mind. She wondered why she never hung out with them. She hadn't asked June or Kate about the woman because that would make her more important than she was. It shouldn't matter. It didn't. She wasn't interested in Cam.

"Earth to Dawn," Kate said with humor in her voice.

Kate's voice brought Dawn back to reality. "What?" She covered as best she could. "Oh sorry, I was just thinking. I was working, but I love bowling even though I haven't had a chance to go in ages. So, yeah sure, I need to finish a couple of things, and then I'll head over."

"Great. We'll see you in a little while then."

"Anything I can bring? A bottle of wine or a six-pack of beer?"

"We never turn down alcohol of any kind, but we'd just love to see you. You don't have to bring anything."

"Okay. Well, then, I'll see you soon." Dawn closed the door behind Kate. *What am I getting myself into?*

Soon Dawn went to the bedroom where she quickly changed into dark jeans and a long-sleeved blouse. She grabbed a bag from the back of the closet. She stopped in the kitchen and opted to take a six-pack of beer. It was more appropriate for a night of steaks and bowling.

Kate had left Cam's front door open, so Dawn walked in, set her bag by the door, and closed the door behind her. She took the beer to the kitchen where she found June.

"Hey, glad you could make it." June wrapped Dawn in a warm embrace.

"Sounds like fun. Should I put this in the fridge?" she asked, raising the six-pack.

"Sure. The opener is on the counter, if you want to pop one open now."

Once Dawn opened a beer, she and June walked out back. Cam stood at the grill watching the steaks. Kate sat under the gazebo chatting with her. Cam looked over as she and June came outside. "Hi, Dawn."

"Hi. Those steaks smell delicious. Thanks for having me over."

"Sure. Glad you could make it." Conversation flowed easily as they shared the meal Cam prepared. Once dinner was finished, everyone pitched in to clean up and then they headed to June's truck to go bowling. When June saw Dawn's bowling bag, she laughed. "Uh-oh, Cam, looks like you might have some serious competition on your hands."

"I enjoy a challenge."

Dawn blushed but didn't respond as she climbed into the backseat with Kate. Certainly Cam was being friendly, not flirting.

Once in their lane, they quickly paired up, Cam and June versus Kate and Dawn, for two games. The first wouldn't count; it was a warm-up. But the second game had teeth. The winning pair would pick the song the losing team had to sing at the karaoke bar attached to the bowling alley. Dawn had never wagered on bowling before, but she figured the worst that could happen was three minutes of humiliation.

Well into the first round, it became obvious the teams were well matched and the next round could get interesting. Dawn hadn't bowled in a long time, and the first round helped her to find her groove again. Kate and June were equally matched, so it came down to a competition between Cam and Dawn. Cam managed to keep it close until the sixth frame. Then Dawn started pulling away. Kate cheered Dawn on as she threw strike after strike. They won handily.

Dawn and Kate shook hands with Cam and June. Dawn smiled as she ever so briefly touched Cam's hand before pulling away. "Good game."

Cam shook her head at Dawn's reaction to her. "That was an outstanding game, Dawn, where did you learn to bowl like that?"

Dawn sat, already pulling off her bowling shoes. She shrugged. "I grew up in a tiny town. Not a lot to do on Friday and Saturday nights."

Kate sat next to Dawn. "So what song should we make them sing?"

"I honestly have no idea. You should pick it."

"No way. We wouldn't have won if it weren't for you. Come on, let's look through the book and pick something good."

Dawn and Kate had their heads close together bent over the song list when Cam and June found them crowded on one side of a small table. They had gotten more beer on their way over. When the two of them sat down, Kate laughed. "This is going to be good."

Dawn said nothing but smiled shyly.

June asked, "So, what would you ladies like us to sing for you?"

Kate slid the song request across the table. Cam and June grinned good-naturedly.

Dawn did all she could to avoid making eye contact with any of them when Kate took the slip of paper to the DJ. They enjoyed the other performers until Cam and June's names were called. As Cam and June stood to walk to the stage, Dawn risked a glance at Cam. Cam winked at Dawn and walked away. Dawn was caught by surprise. She gasped softly and her heart raced. She was busy chastising herself and the next thing she knew the music started. She looked toward the stage and was held in Cam's gaze. Dawn laughed along with Kate as Cam and June hammed it up for the audience as they sang.

Dawn couldn't help but compare Cam to Lori. Lori was wickedly competitive. She suspected Cam was as well in different circumstances. But if tonight was any indication, she was also a very good sport. Her demeanor hadn't changed at all as the game turned in Dawn's favor. She'd never stopped laughing or the teasing banter. Unlike Lori, she had not gotten silently angry and sulked as Dawn took the lead. Not that Lori had ever bothered to go bowling with her, but when they'd played other games Dawn found herself changing the way she played so Lori would have a chance to win. It couldn't be obvious though, or she would have to deal with the aftermath. Dawn hadn't needed to change anything about how she played tonight. She hadn't had a moment of fear about what would happen if she won. She and Kate had beaten Cam and June handily, and she felt good about it. They didn't detract from the victory. In fact they celebrated it with them. They held up their end of the bargain and helped her revel in the win.

❖

Dawn's art reflected her world. Places, people, landscapes, animals, and all other things she found important or inspiring ended up in her pieces. Today, she was working on a simple neighborhood scene. There was the movement of children playing and moms pushing strollers, but also the stillness of people sitting on front porches chatting and flower gardens basking in the sun. She stepped back and studied the canvas. She'd been working for hours and the painting was almost done, but something was missing. She just couldn't figure out what. Perhaps after a break it would come to her. She swirled her brushes in a jar and reached her arms up and stretched her whole body to work out the kinks. After cleaning her brushes, she glanced at her watch and realized it was late afternoon. *It should be cool enough to work in the garden for a while.*

She headed directly to the back door and pulled on her long-sleeve work shirt and floppy hat. She grabbed her gardening bucket and went around the house to weed the beds in the front yard where the shade already crept across the yard.

Dawn noticed too late that Cam was out front working on her motorcycle. There was no gracious exit. She waved and tried to go about her weeding. She tried to ignore Cam, who was less than fifty feet away, but quickly realized that would be impossible as long as she was this close. Instead she decided to engage in neighborly conversation.

Dawn set her tools in her bucket, stood, brushed the dirt from her knees, and peeled off her gloves. Then she headed toward Cam.

Cam smiled. The genuine joy Dawn saw on Cam's face disarmed her. She faltered. She shouldn't get any closer. Cam hadn't made any move to get to know her without June and Kate, and Dawn was grateful for that. She was still uneasy around Cam. There was a pull when she was around, but Dawn didn't want to explore it. She would rather ignore it completely. Perhaps she should just leave it at that. But it felt weird to ignore Cam when she was so close, and if she couldn't talk to her about a common interest, what kind of neighbor was she?

Cam was in the jeans and tight black T-shirt she favored when she wasn't at work. Cam didn't even have to try to be enticing. Dawn shook her head, trying to dispel the thought. "You look happy."

"I am. It's always a pleasure to see you."

Dawn didn't miss the suggestive tone of Cam's remark but chose to ignore it. She nodded toward the bike. "Is something wrong with it?"

"Nah, I just like to tinker sometimes. You know, make sure she stays finely tuned."

"Sure." Dawn ran her hand over the seat. "She's a gorgeous machine."

"You know bikes?"

"Yeah, I grew up with them. All the guys I hung out with had them. I learned about them to keep up. Then I learned to ride. We had a great dirt course just a couple of minutes outside of town. Of course once I got good, I figured out pretty quickly that beating them at their own game wasn't good for maintaining friendships. Luckily, it didn't matter to me. After a while, I just rode for fun. But that was years ago. I haven't ridden in a long time."

"You have so many secrets, my red-haired friend."

Dawn laughed it off. "Not a secret, just something you didn't know."

Cam wiped her hands on the rag she had nearby. "It's a gorgeous day. Why don't you let me take you for a ride? I've got an extra helmet in the garage."

Dawn's heart beat hard in her chest. She was tempted, so tempted. She thought about feeling the power of the engine humming between her legs, the wind rushing by. She missed the sensations of riding a motorcycle, but there was no way she trusted herself to have that experience with Cam. To climb on a bike behind Cam, wrap her arms tightly around her, and feel her heat through the T-shirt she wore. *No way*. Dawn couldn't risk what that might do to her. Simply thinking about it was enough to rev her engine. But temptation did take her as far as glancing at the garage. That's when she saw the truck, Cam's girlfriend's truck. She must be in the house.

"Thanks, but I should get back to my weeding," she said, trying to back away graciously.

"Dawn, what are you scared of?"

"What are you talking about?"

"You're afraid to climb on this bike because it means you would have to get close to me. Why does that scare you?"

Dawn's cheeks flamed. She thought about mentioning the girlfriend. But that made it seem like she was jealous. "Just because I don't feel like a ride today, you make it into something more than it is. It shouldn't surprise me." Okay, that was probably a little harsh.

"What does that mean?" Cam asked.

"Nothing, it doesn't mean anything. Sorry, I just need to get back to my weeding. Enjoy your tinkering."

Dawn turned and walked away before Cam could respond.

Dawn stabbed the spade into the dirt with more force than necessary. *Damn, she irritates me! Just because I don't want to go for a motorcycle ride she thinks I have the hots for her, like she's God's gift to women or something. It couldn't be as simple as I don't feel like going for a ride? So maybe it's true that I don't want to get too close. She has a girlfriend. She shouldn't be flirting with me. Geesh. Just because she offered me a ride on her bike doesn't mean she wants to get in my pants. Maybe she was just being friendly because I expressed an interest in motorcycles. This is just too complicated.*

Dawn yanked weed after weed from the earth and shook the soil from their roots. Her mind whirred in circles. *I was only trying to be a friendly neighbor. Look where that got me, more confused than before. Why the hell does Cam have to be so damn attractive? This isn't getting me anywhere. I just need to go back to work and get my mind off her.* As Dawn flashed back on the piece she'd been painting, it hit her, and she knew what was missing. After she finished weeding, she'd go back into the studio and paint a woman working on her motorcycle. That would complete the painting nicely. But damn if it didn't irritate the hell out of her.

For a second, Cam thought about going after her. *Maybe we should just have it out and get whatever is standing between us out of the way. I'm ready to have that conversation, but I bet Dawn isn't, and without two willing participants we won't get anywhere.*

She let Dawn go. She watched her pull her gloves back on and attack the few weeds that dared sprout since she last tended the front garden. Cam suspected if Dawn wasn't dead set on making a point, she would have simply gone inside and finished her weeding later. She turned back to her bike, whistling. She seemed to be getting under Dawn's skin.

It wasn't actually her goal to irritate Dawn. She simply wanted to get to know her better. The exchange they had just now was the first one Dawn had initiated since the day they met. Cam wanted to figure out a way to learn more about Dawn without scaring her away. They were neighbors, and she didn't want to be at odds with anyone who lived that close.

❖

Cam and Kate had a standing lunch date for Wednesdays when Kate came downtown for classes. Cam was still close with both June and Kate and most often saw them together, but she also regularly got together with each separately to maintain her individual connections. As she waited for Kate, Cam caught herself staring into space again. This wasn't like her. At work, she was usually focused and efficient.

Over the past few weeks, she found her mind wandering at the most inopportune times, during meetings, while talking to her staff, even talking to her boss. This wasn't good. She couldn't stop thinking about Dawn. She intrigued her as few women had. Dawn had developed a quick and easy rapport with June and Kate, but whenever Cam was around it was different. She was quiet and reserved. She wasn't unfriendly. She just seemed to keep her distance. Dawn had a strong, sturdy wall around her, and Cam couldn't seem to get around or through. It puzzled her.

It had always been easy for her to put women at ease, get them talking. Dawn was different. There had to be a way to loosen her reserve. Thankfully, Cam was stopped from meandering down this uncertain path for the eleventeenth time by a knock on her office door.

"Hey," Kate said. "You look totally lost in thought. Where were you?"

Cam locked her computer screen. "Trying to solve a complex problem."

"Do you need some time? I've got a few things I can do."

"No. Maybe a distraction will help. Let's go."

Cam and Kate walked down University Avenue, in the heart of Hillcrest, to one of their favorite Thai restaurants and grabbed a booth.

Once settled, Kate said, "Confession time. You don't daydream, so what's going on?"

"I wish I knew," she said, exhaling deeply and sinking into the bench.

Kate leaned close and put her hand on Cam's arm. "Is everything okay?"

"Yes. Everything's fine. It's just that…this is going to sound strange, but here goes…I can't figure Dawn out."

"What do you mean?" Kate asked.

"Okay, so hear me out. She's intelligent, smokin' hot, talented, funny, and fun to be around, but I don't think she ever goes out. It's like she doesn't have a life outside of her house."

"Maybe she's busy getting ready for her show. Or maybe she goes places when you're at work."

"I thought about that, but she seems to have time to garden and hang out with us when we ask. When you came in I was thinking about how reluctant she is to engage me in conversation. Everything seems to be easy between her and you and June. But between her and me it's…different." Cam groaned. "I sound pathetic."

Kate laughed. "Maybe a little, but I think it's cute. You have a crush." Cam glared at her. "No really, Cam, you have a crush and she's not making it easy for you. When was the last time you had to work to get to know someone?"

Cam stopped to think.

Kate nodded. "Has it ever happened? I know from personal observation you don't usually have any trouble getting women to talk to you. In college, at clubs there were times when women literally fell over themselves to get your attention. Even you and Melanie clicked immediately. Now there's someone who seems indifferent to you and you have no idea what to do with that."

Cam lifted both hands off the table imploringly. "So what do I do?"

"Honestly, June and I both thought you would have asked Dawn out weeks ago."

"I want to, but I can't get a read on her. Not completely. I know I'm in trouble because I'm not even sure she's into women."

"You've never been wrong in that department. Why are you questioning yourself?"

Cam shook her head. "I don't know. I can't put my finger on it. There's just something different about her. I can't stop thinking about her, and I want to know her story, her whole story, but she resists. She doesn't share anything about herself. She'll talk about her art or gardening, but personal stuff—that's off limits. I've tried to breach that divide with no success. None. In fact, she downright refuses my every suggestion."

Kate shrugged. "The way I see it, you have a couple of options. You can wait and see if she warms up to you. Or you can ask her out and get an answer pretty quickly on how she feels about you. Since we're not in junior high, I'm not going to offer to find out if she likes you."

Cam laughed at the absurdity of Kate's last comment. "Right, I'll take it from here."

"I'm certain you will. I'm always here when you need to talk."

"I know, thanks. Anyway, enough about me, what's happening in your life? How are your new dance classes going?"

"Things are going okay. Slower than I expected. I'm still trying to drum up more interest. I know there have to be more women out there who want to learn swing dancing. I've put flyers up at the Center and I've gotten a few calls, but interest seems low. Hopefully, the class that starts in three weeks will fill. Don't you know anyone who would want to take dance lessons?"

"I'm not sure, maybe. Let me send some emails. Do you have an extra flyer with all the information?"

"Sure." Kate pulled a colorful piece of paper out of her shoulder bag. "Here you go. I'll email you one, too. You should think about taking the class too."

"Why? I already know how to swing."

"I know. So come for fun and to help me. I can always use an extra set of hands. Most people need a lot of attention when they're first learning. Besides, you could come right after work. It's just down the street. It will get you out of the house and maybe your mind off other things."

"I'll think about it." A distraction might be exactly what she needed.

Kate nodded. "That's all I can ask."

Chapter Four

Cam glanced at the clock by the television when she heard a knock at the door. Both dogs stood facing the door, ears up and tails wagging and low barks alerting her about the soon-to-be intruder. She turned off the iron she was using to prepare her clothes for the week. "Jack, Mozz, settle." Cam opened the door to see Dawn. "Well, hello." She smiled but noticed something wasn't right. "What's wrong?"

"If I remember right, you're in IT. Please tell me you know something about computers."

"I do. What's going on?"

"I've been working on a proposal for several weeks, and it's due by tomorrow morning. All of the sudden, my computer died. I turned it off last night and this morning I can't get it to turn back on. I've called everyone I can think of who knows computers and I can't get hold of anyone. You're my last hope. I'm sorry for interrupting your evening, but I don't know what else to do."

Cam didn't hesitate. "Let's go take a look."

Walking across the yard, Dawn turned to Cam, her relief obvious. "Thank you so much."

"I haven't done anything yet. Let's wait and see what's going on."

As Dawn led Cam through her house, Cam took a quick look around. She had lived next door for almost two months, and even though Dawn had been to her house several times when June and Kate were over, Cam had never been invited into Dawn's home. As she followed Dawn, she caught a glimpse of the same pictures that captivated June on her first visit. Even with the abbreviated view, she knew June hadn't been exaggerating when she said Dawn's work was marvelous. Cam trailed Dawn through another doorway and stopped, awestruck. She was surrounded by art in all shapes and sizes and mediums. She could see Dawn's talent spread across the canvasses. "Wow."

"Cam, the computer is over here."

Dawn's voice broke through Cam's thoughts, and she managed to turn away from the canvas she was studying. "Right, okay, let's see what we have."

Right away, Cam noticed that while the monitor had power the computer did not. She checked the connection and found it secure. Cam glanced up at Dawn. "Do you have another power cord?"

"Um, only the one on the other computer."

"Where's that?"

"In the other room." Cam followed Dawn.

Cam retrieved the power cord from the computer in the living room and returned to the studio. She replaced the power cord, unplugged the monitor, and plugged the computer into the spot where the monitor had been. So she knew she was using a known good cable into a known good outlet, still no power on the computer. "Okay, I think your power supply is toast. I eliminated several possibilities, but we need some parts."

"That doesn't sound good. Can you fix it?"

"Not tonight. I need a replacement power supply and no store is still open that will have one." When Cam saw Dawn's crestfallen face, she added, "But I might have a workaround so you can get your proposal sent out. No promises though."

"I'd appreciate anything you can do."

The expression on Dawn's face made Cam want to leap tall buildings to help her. She made quick work of removing the remaining cables from the computer in the studio and took off the cover. She quickly disconnected the hard drive and she stood with it and the extra power cord in her hands.

Dawn stared at the innards of her computer. She looked at Cam uncertainly. "This looks bad. What are you going to do with that?"

"I'm going to try to make it a secondary drive on your computer in the living room so you can access your files." Seeing Dawn confused expression, she asked, "Trust me?"

"Do I have a choice?"

Cam's eyes narrowed. "You always have a choice."

Dawn started to speak and then stopped. Finally, she said, "Please do whatever you have to."

Cam wondered what she'd stopped herself from saying. "Okay, let's go."

They made their way back into the living room. Cam disconnected the components from the computer and removed the cover; she checked the jumper on the hard drive from the studio computer, and connected it to a cable inside the machine. She replaced the cover, then reconnected all the wires and power cord. "Well, here goes our best shot."

Dawn held her breath when Cam pushed the power button. She breathed a small sigh of relief when the machine powered on.

"That's not the tricky part," Cam explained. "We need the computer to recognize the hard drive from your work computer."

Cam knew what she was doing and was confident in what she did. Soon, the familiar screens appeared on the monitor. In no time at all a file was opening on the screen and Cam pushed the chair back from the desk. She nodded toward the screen. "Is this the proposal you were working on?"

Dawn's gaze flew back to the screen. "Yes. Oh my God, yes." She pulled Cam into a quick, hard hug. "I don't know how I can thank you. This is amazing. You have no idea how much this means to me."

"You seemed pretty desperate," Cam said.

"So, you have some ideas on how I can thank you for rescuing me?"

"I do. I'm hoping you can help me with my yard. It's in desperate need of color. Next to yours, it's plain and inadequate. Would you mind helping me with a plan for my yard and go with me to help me pick out some plants and stuff?"

"Really? You want me to help you with your yard?" Dawn asked excitedly.

"If I had known how thrilled you would be, I'd have asked ages ago."

"I'd love to. I've been trying to think of a way to get my hands in your yard since the first day I saw it. It has so much potential. Of course I can help you with it."

Cam was surprised by Dawn's enthusiasm. "Great, then it's a deal. I'm working from home tomorrow. Are you free to go to the nursery in the morning?"

"Sounds like a plan." Dawn's mind seemed to race ahead with what she could do with Cam's yard.

"Great. Go ahead and send off your email and I'll clean up the mess in the other room." Cam walked to the studio. First, she did what she needed to do and noted the make and model of the computer before squaring it away. She liked to finish what she started, so she would find a new power supply and replace it for Dawn tomorrow. Then, she turned to do what she had wanted to do since the moment she entered the studio. She moved from piece to piece, taking in Dawn's work. The way Dawn created movement in water when she painted streams, rivers, and the ocean was splendid. But the overall effect of her art was breathtaking.

Cam reached a piece that stopped her in her tracks. At first glance, it was a simple scene of a turbulent sea during a storm. The harshness of the waves battering the rocks of the cliff was powerful, almost painful. As she stepped closer to take in the details, she noticed the lighthouse but no light shined. No beacon to navigate safely. It made her feel…sad, despondent, and vulnerable. So many people were going to get hurt.

After she finished sending off the proposal, Dawn returned to the studio and found Cam staring at one of her paintings. She stopped at the threshold and studied Cam. She had never seen anyone look at her work in quite the same way. The intense concentration emphasized the strong angles of Cam's chiseled face. She was overwhelmed by Cam's unguarded expression.

Dawn painted for herself. It was something she was compelled to do, but seeing the effect her art had on others was always a thrill, which is why she occasionally agreed to show her work. However, in all the years she had shared her art with the world, she had never seen the look she saw in Cam's eyes. It made her heart race. She moved quietly to see what piece captured Cam's attention. When Cam turned, she hadn't had time to control her thoughts or feelings. As her gaze locked with Dawn's, the raw emotion took Dawn's breath away.

Dawn felt like she had intruded on a private moment. "I'm sorry if I disturbed you," she said softly.

"Don't be. It's your house. I was just appreciating your work. It's…expressive and passionate. The intensity pulls you in. It's very powerful."

"Thank you." Dawn focused on the picture Cam had been studying, and her heart skipped a beat. She hadn't shown this piece to anyone. She wasn't ready to until recently. She was considering putting it in her upcoming show. It had been sitting in her studio since she painted it more than two years ago. Cam was the first person to view it. Now the expression Dawn saw on Cam's face was more special because the emotions still swirling in Cam's dark eyes reflected the intensity Dawn felt when she painted it.

Dawn looked back up. Cam studied her face just as she had studied Cam's moments earlier. She felt her cheeks flush. She and Cam stared intently into one another's eyes. For the first time, Dawn didn't look away. She didn't want to.

Cam moved to Dawn and lifted the back of her hand to Dawn's cheek and stroked it. "Do you always do this when someone compliments your work?"

Dawn pulled back but didn't drop her eyes. "No."

Cam closed the distance once more. "Maybe one day you will tell me about this piece and share what or who caused you such anguish."

Dawn's breathing hitched as Cam hit the mark of the emotion that inspired that piece. She left the comment unanswered. Everything that came to mind seemed inadequate.

Dawn figured out Cam's intention the second before it happened, but she didn't stop it. Her first instinct was to push her away. She raised her hands to Cam's shoulders but didn't follow through. Cam held her lightly, tenderly. She lost herself in the kiss. Cam's mouth was soft but firm. The warmth sent shivers down Dawn's spine. When Cam's tongue gently pressed for entry, Dawn didn't hesitate. She opened her lips, and as Cam's tongue met hers, her insides melted from the heat.

Dawn thrust her hands into Cam's hair, adjusted the angle of her head, and kissed her harder. There was no thought. Lust shot through her, and she craved more…more tongue, more skin, more—

Cam's dogs barking loudly finally penetrated her short-circuiting brain. She pulled back. "Cam…"

"Just ignore them. They'll stop in a minute."

Dawn stepped back as realization crept in. *What have I done?* Another step away from Cam. "They're not stopping. You should probably go check on them."

"I could come back."

"That's not necessary." Dawn was trying really hard to remain calm.

"Okay. I'll see you in the morning to go to the garden center."

Dawn walked Cam to the door and shut it behind her. She wasn't sure how long she stood there staring at the door. *Whoa.* She hadn't expected the kiss, not really. A part of her had been worried something like this would happen from the day she had met Cam, but she'd kept her distance. Dawn started to think maybe it was all in her head.

Then it hit her. This was the first time she allowed herself to be alone with Cam for more than a few minutes. *That's not fair. True, she kissed you, but you did nothing to stop her. You even participated. You can't blame her for that without accepting your part in it. Okay, but I'm not attached. What about the blonde Cam is with?*

Dawn was dismayed. *How can she kiss me while she's seeing someone else? Why does it surprise me? That's one of the reasons I kept my distance. How dare her.* She didn't know Cam that well, but somehow this just didn't feel like something she would do. Maybe she and the blonde had broken up. Cam had never mentioned her. Maybe it was all in Dawn's head. Even with the cloud of confusion Dawn worked herself into, she could still feel the heat of Cam's lips on hers.

❖

As Cam crossed the front yard and walked into her house, she thought about the emotion in Dawn's art and about the kiss. The intensity of the kiss didn't surprise her. She knew it would be incredible. It also didn't surprise her that she very much wanted to walk back in there and finish what she started. But she knew Dawn wasn't ready for that and it would break every rule Cam had to push Dawn before she was ready. Even kissing her as she just had bent the rules because she sensed Dawn was not open to it. She's just wasn't sure why. After more than two months of holding herself back whenever Dawn was around, she had to push just a little. She knew it would be immeasurably more difficult to restrain herself in the future. Now that she had a taste, she wanted more, much more.

Cam hadn't anticipated the willingness and eagerness of Dawn's response. She sensed Dawn's moment of hesitation, and then Dawn wrapped her arms around Cam's shoulders and pressed her body against Cam. She'd almost lost herself in the kiss. It had taken everything she had to step back from the edge, to move away from Dawn. She didn't question it was the right thing to do. Sometimes she wished it wasn't so important to her to do the right thing.

What disquieted Cam was her reaction to Dawn. She hadn't felt that intensity from a simple kiss since Melanie died two years ago. Melanie was the love of her life. She found that one of a kind love early and knew no one could replace her. So what was it about Dawn that had her so intrigued?

Chapter Five

Dawn's usual cheery morning mood was tempered by the events of the previous evening. When she remembered her deal with Cam she covered her head with a pillow. She softened. *A deal's a deal.* She would help Cam pick out some plants and give her some ideas for arranging them. Then she'd leave her to execute it. Reluctantly, Dawn climbed out of bed to shower and start the day. Her mood lightened as she anticipated a morning at the garden center, a place full of hope and new budding delight.

As she pulled on her shoes, the doorbell chimed. She glanced in the mirror above her dresser, satisfied she had successfully camouflaged her rough night. She grabbed her purse and walked into the living room. She braced herself and opened her front door. *Damn, Cam is gorgeous. Breathe.*

Cam stood on her porch in jeans and a T-shirt, her dark hair still damp from the shower with that cute crooked grin lighting her strong features. She held salvation in the form of to-go coffee mugs. "I made us coffee for the road." She thrust a mug toward Dawn.

"Thank you."

Cam crossed the threshold, and with her now free hand, she reached up and rubbed her thumb across the smudges under Dawn's eye. "Rough night?"

Dawn steeled herself against Cam's tender touch and didn't react visibly. Dawn met Cam's questioning look and shrugged. "Yeah. There was still a lot to do once you left." With that, Dawn walked out the door waiting for Cam to follow before she locked up. Dawn was elusive. She didn't want to tread into the same territory they'd explored last night. There were too many questions or maybe just too many women. Still, being this close to Cam drove her crazy. She wanted to be mad at her, but at the same time, she wanted Cam to kiss her again. She was mad at herself for even going there.

"Let's take the truck so we have plenty of room for whatever we pick up," Cam said.

The blonde's truck? Is she still at your place, sleeping in your bed? Dawn responded without looking at Cam, her jaw tight. "Okay."

Cam glanced sideways at Dawn trying to gauge her mood. Something seemed off this morning, but that was status quo for her and Dawn. Having never spent time with Dawn this early, Cam couldn't decide if she was grumpy or just not a morning person. Dawn was quiet while she climbed into the cab and Cam backed out of the driveway. Cam contemplated turning on the radio and decided against it. She drove for a while in silence wondering if Dawn would say what was on her mind. When she didn't, Cam spoke. She wanted to confront any issue head-on. "Dawn, are you okay? I could guess why you're upset, but I would rather you tell me."

"You really want to talk about this right now?"

"I do. Why are you so upset?"

"Well, for starters, you kissed me."

Before responding Cam pulled the truck into the parking lot of the nursery and parked in the first spot she found at the rear of the lot. She turned so she could fully face Dawn.

"I did and you kissed me back."

Confusion flashed in Dawn's eyes. She released her seat belt. "I know that and I take full responsibility for my part, but I'm not involved with someone else. I'm not the one who is cheating on my girlfriend." Dawn pushed the door open and hopped out before Cam could process what she said.

Cam tried to figure out what Dawn was talking about. She had never seen Dawn so angry. Eventually, she got out of the truck and headed into the nursery to find Dawn. She spotted her amidst the sea of red annuals. Dawn was surrounded by pots of flowers and was obviously in her element. *She is so beautiful.* Even with Dawn incoherent this morning, she was striking.

Cam didn't hide her approach. She didn't want to sneak up on Dawn as she browsed the selection. "Dawn?"

Dawn glanced at Cam warily. "What?"

"I have no idea what you're talking about. I'm not involved with anyone and haven't been for a long time. I do not have a girlfriend."

Dawn shook her head, defeated. "At least have the decency not to lie to me. I saw you two together last month."

"I have absolutely no idea who you're talking about."

"Oh, come on, Cam. The day after you moved in a beautiful blonde was over at your house. You walked to the truck arm in arm, the same truck we came here in today." Dawn turned away.

Cam stopped her. "Whoa! Dawn, you're confused. It's not what you think it is."

Dawn frowned. "It never is."

Cam shook her head. "I feel like I'm being blamed for someone else's sins. At least let me explain."

"What's the point? You don't owe me an explanation."

Cam saw that Dawn's eyes were no longer full of anger. She was hurt. The same hurt Cam had seen come and go over the last couple of weeks was out of the shadows. She saw the pain Dawn translated to the canvas in her eyes. Anguish. She realized this went much deeper than her. "Dawn." Cam stopped. She couldn't ask for more than Dawn was ready to give. "I'm telling you the truth. It's up to you whether you believe me or not. Cindy, that's her name, the woman you saw me with last month. Cindy is a friend. She has never been anything more than a great friend. She's more of a big sister really. I went to live with her when I was in high school because I wanted to stay here to finish school while my parents lived out of the country. I don't know what you think you saw, but when Cindy and I were walking to the truck she was telling me how proud she was of me for getting the house and some other changes I made in my life recently. I've known Cindy longer than I've known Kate and June. She's been there for me through some hard times. She and her wife, Lynn, watched my dogs while I moved in.

"Cindy and Lynn had the truck, my truck, in case either of them needed to take the boys somewhere. I didn't need it while I was moving, and it was easier to have it out of the way. Cindy brought the truck over so she could get the tour of the house. Then I took her back to her place and picked up my dogs. When the boys and I got home, I parked the truck in the garage because I only use it when I'm doing something that won't work on the bike. I love Cindy, but she and I have never been and will never be 'involved.'"

Dawn made eye contact with Cam and whispered, "I'm sorry." Then she dropped her gaze and felt the petals on the flowers in front of her.

Cam studied the top of Dawn's head. The smart thing to do would probably be to walk away and let Dawn regain her composure. But this was the closest she had come to figuring out what happened to Dawn. She had to ask the questions that had been rolling around in her head for weeks. "Dawn, what happened? Who hurt you?"

She kept her head lowered and shook her head slightly. "It doesn't matter. It was a long time ago."

Cam was frustrated by Dawn's response, but she also recognized the defeat she heard. If she pushed she could probably get the answers she sought, but she'd also lose the trust she sought to build with Dawn. Suddenly, the middle of the nursery didn't feel like a good place for a heartfelt talk. She relented. "Okay, for now."

The relief was evident on Dawn's face. "So, let me show you some ideas I have for your yard."

As they moved in and out of the rows of tables with various plants, Dawn's mood transformed while she discussed the needs of different plants and where each might thrive in Cam's yard. The angst and vulnerability she had fluctuated between all morning had dissipated. Among the plants, Dawn seemed rejuvenated. It was almost as though the argument never happened. Cam lost herself in Dawn's passion. Her porcelain cheeks flushed with pleasure as she talked about the possibilities: annuals, perennials, evergreens, shrubs, and even statuary. "So, what do you think?" Dawn laughed in delight at Cam's overwhelmed bafflement. "Sorry, I get a little carried away when I talk about gardening."

Cam recovered quickly. "I think I have an idea." She turned and disappeared down the adjoining aisle then returned pushing a flat cart. "I think the best thing to do is for you decide what will look best. I leave myself in your very capable hands," she said, making a show of bowing to Dawn.

Dawn searched Cam's face looking for hidden meaning before responding. Satisfied with what she saw, or didn't see, Dawn rubbed her hands together in excitement. "This is exhilarating." She giggled and started loading the cart carefully, placing plants in groupings.

"I guess it's a good thing we brought *my* truck."

After Cam paid, one of the nursery staff helped them load everything into the truck.

Dawn climbed in and Cam started the engine. "There's just one more place we need to stop. I thought we could get you a new power supply, so we can get the computer in your studio back up and running."

"You don't have to do that."

"A deal's a deal. Besides, I do what I say I'm going to do, and I always finish what I start."

Dawn could not think of an adequate response and felt the lameness of her reply. "Okay." She had never been in a store dedicated to computers and their components. She had no idea where to begin. Luckily, Cam seemed to know exactly where to go.

Cam quickly found the aisle they needed and took out the piece of paper she carried in her pocket with the information she needed to get the right model power supply. Cam apparently found the proper package and turned to Dawn. "This is what you need."

"If you say so."

The drive home was quiet. As Cam pulled into the driveway, she broke the silence. "If you can help me unload all this stuff quickly, then I can hook up the new power supply so you can get back to work."

"Sounds like a deal," Dawn said.

They worked silently unloading the supplies from the truck into the backyard, Dawn pointing to various spots to indicate where the bigger items should be placed. Then they walked to Dawn's front door.

Dawn let them into the house and turned. She felt foolish. Cam's explanation at the nursery made perfect sense. Her own insecurities concocted the whole relationship between Cam and Cindy. It was safer for her to think Cam was unavailable. It wasn't fair to Cam to be mad at her for something she obviously wasn't guilty of, but she wasn't sure how to make things right.

"Listen, Cam, I owe you an apology. I jumped to conclusions. I doubted you for reasons that had nothing to do with you. I'm sorry."

"So make it up to me. Let me make you dinner."

"You've made me dinner before."

"No. We've had dinner, but June and Kate were there. As much as I love them, I am hoping you and I can have dinner alone."

"That sounds like a date." Dawn made a statement, but it was a question too.

"It was meant to."

"I can't do that, Cam. I'm not available."

"You said you weren't seeing anyone."

"I'm not."

"Then I don't understand. Why can't we have dinner?"

"I'm not interested in dating women," Dawn said resolutely.

Cam laughed humorlessly. "You could have fooled me by your reaction to the kiss yesterday."

"That's chemistry and we certainly have that, but I don't date anymore."

Cam moved closer to her and Dawn barely resisted the urge to back away. "What? Why? What happened?"

"It doesn't matter."

Cam gently put a hand on Dawn's elbow. "I care that you're hurting."

Dawn carefully removed Cam's hand and backed up, creating distance between them. Then she shook her head. "That's history, Cam. It's in the past."

"No, it's not. You might like to think it's history, but it's affecting your present. That makes it a current issue. If you don't want to go on a date with me, fine, I can accept that, but at least be honest about the reasons." Cam turned and headed for the studio.

Dawn felt the frustration radiating off Cam. Even though she had never seen this side of her, she wasn't frightened. She didn't know if it was best to keep her distance, try to placate, or something else. She opted for staying out of her way. It might have been cowardly, but since Dawn couldn't give Cam what she wanted, it felt like the safest option.

After Cam finished replacing the power supply and returned the respective hard drives to the proper computers, she headed for the door.

Dawn stopped her by laying her hand on her arm. "Cam, wait."

Cam turned back to Dawn. "Why?"

Dawn saw more than frustration on Cam's face. She saw hurt.

The hurt threw her. "I just wanted to say…thank you."

Cam nodded curtly. "You're welcome." She turned and left.

Dawn stared at the door. *What just happened?*

As Cam closed Dawn's door behind her, she saw June pulling up next door. She raised her hand in greeting and walked over.

"Hey, what are you up to?" June said playfully, suggestively even, but frowned as she got close enough to see Cam's face. "Uh-oh, what happened?"

"Nothing," Cam answered shortly. She struggled to get her emotions under control. "I need coffee. Want some?"

"Do you even have to ask?"

June plopped down onto one of the bar stools at the island and Cam filled the mugs. Cam doctored June's coffee the way she liked it and slid the cup across the counter to her. Cam leaned back against the counter and took a sip of her own black coffee.

"Cam?"

June's voice pulled Cam back from her own distracted thoughts. "Hmm…"

"Are you okay?"

Cam smirked. She couldn't help it. There wasn't a question for June that something was wrong. She knew Cam too well to not know when something upset her. It felt good to have friends who knew her so well. June didn't need to dance around her feelings because the two of them had been through so much together. She also knew June would wait however long it took for her to be ready to talk about whatever troubled her.

"I kissed Dawn."

"Just now?"

"No. Last night."

"And you're just leaving her house this morning?" June's mouth quirked up with the thought.

"No," Cam said with resignation. "Let me start from the beginning."

"Okay."

"Dawn came over last night in a panic because her computer died while she was finishing an important file she'd been working on for weeks. I agreed to take a look to see if there was anything I could do."

"Sure."

"Dawn was so excited when I found a work-around that she hugged me."

"You sound surprised. She's hugged you before," June said as if trying to figure out a puzzle.

Cam frowned. "No, June, she hasn't. She hugs you and Kate every time she sees you. But she has never touched me in any way other than a handshake or high five, and even that is a rare occurrence."

"That's ridiculous."

"Think about it. When have you ever seen Dawn come within three feet of me?"

June opened her mouth to respond but stopped.

"Exactly."

"She thanked me again and asked how she could pay me back. So I asked her to help me with my yard. You know, put some color in it, and help me plan things. You would think I just gave her the best present ever. She was so excited. I have never seen her show that kind of emotion."

"So was that when you kissed her?"

"No. I told her to send her email and I went into the studio to clean up the computer mess I'd left in there. While she worked, I started looking at her paintings. I was completely engrossed in her work and I have no idea how long it was before Dawn came and found me."

"I can only imagine. She's incredibly talented. There's a lot going on there, and it's all on the canvases."

"Yeah, she's amazing. Anyway, I'm looking at this incredible painting full of emotion and intensity, and it feels like I'm looking into her soul. When she came in, I swear there was this moment, just a moment, when I thought she would let me in. That she would open a door in that wall she has so dutifully built."

"What happened?" June asked softly.

"I couldn't let the moment pass. I kissed her. It was intense and amazing. But then the dogs were barking so loud, I had to check on them. Then this morning, I picked her up because we made plans to go to the nursery. She was standoffish and quiet at first, but she finally told me what was bothering her. Turns out she had seen Cindy and me together last month and thought we were together. So she accused me of cheating on Cindy by kissing her."

"But that's not what's wrong."

"No. I wish she would have asked me about it, but I can understand her anger given what she thought the situation was. Once I explained, Dawn apologized, but when I asked her about her reasons for jumping to that conclusion, she shut me out again. I let it go. The middle of the nursery didn't seem like the place to dig into all that. We managed to finish up at the nursery and get the part for her computer without further incident. When we got back she apologized again. I told her she could make it up to me by letting me cook her dinner. Things didn't go so well. She turned me down cold. When I asked why, she told me she doesn't date, like at all. I asked her to explain that and she shut down."

"It's not her turning down the date that upset you. It's that she won't tell you what happened."

"I don't get it. Most women, when you show genuine interest in what's bothering them, will open up. I don't know why she doesn't trust me."

"Cam," June started softly, "Dawn is not 'most women,' you know that. Why should she trust you? How would she know she can?" Cam started to defend her honor. "Hold on. I know she can. You know and so do your friends. Even the women you've dated would tell her so, but how does Dawn know it? From everything you've said, it sounds like Dawn was hurt badly. I feel awful for not seeing it myself. Maybe it scares her that you see it. Obviously, it's not something she feels comfortable sharing, and the fact that you see it probably unsettles her. Trusting you might mean letting out painful, even buried memories.

"Look, Cam, when I got here today you were upset, but when I asked you what was wrong you said 'nothing.' I didn't press because I knew you would tell me when you were ready. That's how it has always been with us. You don't talk about something until you're ready, and nobody can change that."

"Yeah."

"So, maybe that's what is happening with Dawn. Maybe she's not ready. Maybe she needs to see you as a friend, as trustworthy, before anything else. Or maybe she just doesn't like you. I don't think that's it. I have seen the way she watches you when she thinks nobody's looking. Obviously, there's something about you that she's wary of given her responses so far. But it might not have anything to do with *you*. She knows you can see something she spends a lot of time and energy trying to hide. Can you think for a moment how that would make you feel?"

"I guess if someone was able to see beyond my defenses, I would feel…vulnerable. That's the only word I can come up with."

"Yeah, me too, maybe if you give her some time she'll come around. Try not to take it personally. I know how hard that might be for you, but remember how hard it must be for her. Maybe that will help."

Cam nodded, trying to process the conversation. "Thanks for the ear. I mean it. Thanks for listening and helping me see this from another perspective."

"Any time. Speaking of time, I'm supposed to go over to Dawn's in fifteen minutes to talk about the picture for Kate. Do you want me to cancel?"

"Of course not. Whatever is between Dawn and me shouldn't interfere with what you two have going on." Cam had no doubt that her conversation with June would remain between them. June would never share her confidences with anyone other than Kate, which she was fine with.

"June?"

"Yes?"

"Will you…will you just make sure she's okay?"

"Of course I will."

"Thank you."

CHAPTER SIX

Dawn had been too distracted to put paint to canvas since Cam left. She had gone to her studio several times with the intention of painting, but each time left the room without even preparing her palette or selecting her brushes. She was currently using the excuse that she had an appointment and needed to keep an eye on the time. But she admitted to herself that she was too churned up from her conversation with Cam to do much of anything. As a result, she spent the time answering emails and looking over design ideas. When the doorbell rang, the nerves in her stomach jumped to her throat and she glanced at her watch. *Right on time.*

As she walked to the door, she didn't know how she would be received. June was Cam's best friend. No doubt she would know if Cam was upset, and Dawn had seen her pull into Cam's driveway just after she'd left earlier.

When she opened the door to June, she was welcomed into a warm embrace. "Hi, Dawn."

Dawn returned the hug. "Hi. How are you?"

"I'm good. I decided to stop by Cam's early so I wouldn't be late for our meeting."

Dawn was still cautious. "Oh." June said nothing further. "Come on in. How's Kate? I've been meaning to invite you two to dinner."

"Kate's good. I thought you couldn't cook."

"I can't, but I'm great at making reservations and picking up takeout."

June's strong laugh had the last of Dawn's nerves easing. "We'll have to do that."

"Great. Shall we get started?"

"Yes, I'm so excited."

June followed Dawn into the studio. "Would you like some coffee or something?"

"No, thanks. I just had some at Cam's," she said easily.

"Okay. Well, let me show you what I've got. Based on the ideas we talked about last time, I sketched out a couple of ideas. Why don't we look through them and you can tell me what you like and don't like about them. I mean that. Tell me when you don't like something. It's as important as what you do like. We want this piece to be something special for Kate, but it will be in your home and you should enjoy it too."

"I hadn't thought about it like that. Okay," June said.

"Good." Dawn pulled her sketchbook from the drafting table and flipped to the pages she was looking for. "Okay, start with this one. Then look at the next two. Then we can go through them together and discuss them. But first I want you to just look at them and see if any of these is what you are looking for."

June took her time with each sketch, all three different places of importance to Kate and June—the beach where they'd declared their love for each other, Balboa Park where they'd gone to walk on their first date, and the caves in La Jolla where June had proposed to Kate. "Dawn, they're all amazing. I don't know how I'll decide."

Dawn smiled. "That's what I'm here for. So let's talk through them. Look at the first one again and tell me what you feel when you look at it. What stands out to you? Is there anything about the picture you like or don't like?"

They went through this exercise with each sketch. All the while, Dawn took notes. Then she talked to June about what colors she would use and the size of the painting.

"These are incredible. I think whatever you paint will be right for Kate and me. I leave myself completely in your talented hands."

Dawn had heard variations of this before and easily accepted the challenge. "All right, I'll give you a call when it's ready. In the mean time, we should go out to dinner."

"Absolutely. Let me check with Kate and I'll let you know what our schedule looks like and we can set something up, maybe late next week?"

"That would be great. I'm pretty open, especially if I have a day's notice."

"Excellent. Now that those things are taken care of, there's something I want to talk to you about."

Dawn's heart started beating fast and she got butterflies in her stomach. *Uh-oh, here it comes. This is where June lambasts me for upsetting Cam.*

"Relax, it's nothing bad. At least I don't think it is. I'm sure it won't surprise you Cam told me about your…misunderstanding. She was pretty upset when she left here this morning."

"I know. I feel badly that I jumped to conclusions."

June shrugged. "I might have thought the same thing in your position, but what I don't understand is, even if you didn't feel comfortable asking Cam who Cindy was, why didn't you ask Kate or me?"

"You're Cam's friends."

"I'm your friend too, so is Kate."

"But you were both Cam's friend first, so your loyalty is to her."

"So you think because Kate and I knew Cam before you, we would cover for her?"

"Yeah, maybe. How would I know?"

"That's a good point. We have been friends for a very long time and through a lot together. I forget that can be overwhelming for somebody new. But let me be very clear here. Neither Kate nor I would ever lie for Cam. First, she would never want us to, and second, there would be no reason to. Cam is one of the most honest and decent people I've ever met. If she ever found out that one of us had lied for her, she would come undone."

"Okay…then let me ask you this. Why isn't she dating anyone?"

"Well, since Melanie she just hasn't dated a whole lot."

"Melanie?"

"Cam hasn't mentioned Melanie?"

"No."

"Hmm…then I should let her tell you."

Dawn was about to point out that June just told her that she could ask her or Kate anything about Cam, but Dawn had her own secrets and would want the same discretion from her friends. "I understand."

"Anyway, I wanted to clear the air."

"I appreciate it."

❖

"Cam!" June yelled just before she slammed the door.

Cam rushed out of her office alarmed by June's tone. "What? What happened?"

"You tell me. How can you be upset with Dawn for not telling you about whatever is in her past when you haven't told her about Melanie?"

Cam's defenses flared. "What are you talking about? What did you say to her?"

"She asked why you weren't dating anyone, and I said that since Melanie you haven't dated a whole lot. When she didn't know who Mel was, I told her I had to let you tell her in your own time. She said she understood."

Cam slumped into a chair.

June took a seat on the couch. "Cam, what's going on?"

Cam scrubbed her hands down her face. "I don't know. I mean, I haven't felt anything like this since I first met Melanie. Then I feel bad because Dawn's not Melanie. I guess I feel guilty. But it doesn't matter does it? Dawn's not interested. I should just leave her alone and go on with my life, right? It would certainly be less complicated."

"Is that what you want to do, forget you ever met Dawn? You could ignore your next-door neighbor, pretend she doesn't exist. That's one strategy."

"Yes. No. I don't know. I don't think that's even possible. I already think about her all the time. It seems unlikely that's going to change, but it needs to. I need to."

"And that's the real problem. You feel guilty for thinking about Dawn because you used to spend all your time thinking about Melanie, even after she died."

"Melanie's the love of my life."

"Melanie is gone. She was your first true love. She would want you to be happy. Why do you feel like you can't move on? She wouldn't want you to suffer if you have a chance at happiness again, and you can't get there if you don't try."

Once Cam left for work the next morning, Dawn let herself into Cam's yard and started refining the design she had worked on in her head during the night. She wanted to do this for Cam. She just wasn't sure why. She greeted the curious dogs who welcomed her familiar scent and then got to work. The dogs followed her for a while to see if she was playing a game that included them, but soon gave up and lay down to snooze.

When she and Cam unloaded the truck the day before, Cam helped her put things in the general areas where Dawn indicated based on her plan. This morning she spent some time making adjustments, fine-tuning her plans, and then went to work preparing the soil, planting, and mulching. By midmorning, Dawn stood and stretched. The sun was high overhead as she surveyed the yard to inspect her work. She was pleased with her progress.

The small beds around the perimeter of the patio were dotted with color and different textures. Before she could continue, she needed to talk with Cam about getting a few more things. She'd also realized she needed to add some trees and shrubs to create elevation and interest in the sides of the yard. The main part of the yard would remain open for the dogs to run and play, but by the time Dawn's plan was completed it would look like a completely different space. She laughed at herself. She was giddy to have a fresh garden canvas to work with.

Chapter Seven

Dawn looked at her sister, Ali, who sat across from her on the couch. An open bottle of wine sat on the table between them. They each had a full glass. "I can't believe you're here," she gushed.

"You know I like to surprise you, sweetie. I couldn't miss your show," Ali said.

"I'm happy you're here, but what about work and school?"

Ali shook her head. "Not a problem. I worked it all out. I wanted to come see my big sister's show, so I made it happen." Ali worked hard in her program, and she was very competent.

"Okay. I'll stop worrying about it then."

Ali raised her glass. "I'll drink to that."

Dawn raised her glass in salute and then took a sip. "So fill me in. What have you been up to? It feels like forever since we've had a real conversation. Life's been so busy."

They talked late into the night catching up on each other's lives. Dawn filled Ali in on the pieces she was finishing up for the show. Ali talked about her classes and her job at the hospital. "Do you still love the research project you're working on with your professor?" Dawn asked.

"I do. It's fascinating to be able to see the different ways the human brain works. All that they're capable of."

"I bet it is. I'm glad you're enjoying it. But I still kinda hate that you don't live closer."

"I know, but I really like Seattle. Who knows where I'll end up after I'm done with school? Maybe I'll be somewhere a bit closer. At least I'm not back East like Mom and Dad."

"You have a good point. Please don't ever move that far away."

"I won't say never, but I would like to stay close to you if it's possible."

Finally heading to bed after three in the morning, Dawn yawned sleepily. "Thanks for coming, Ali. I'm glad you're here. I love you."

"You're welcome. I love you, too. Good night," Ali said as she walked to the guest room.

"G'night," Dawn replied softly. As she drifted off to sleep, she thought about the surprise she'd left in Cam's yard and she wondered if she'd seen it yet.

❖

After just three hours of sleep, Dawn woke up energized. She peeked into the guest room and checked on her sister. Leaving Ali to sleep, she slipped out of bed and headed for the kitchen. She was thrilled Ali was here. Her spirits lifted the moment she'd seen Ali standing on her porch. It was just like Ali not to tell her she was coming, even going so far as to arrive at her front door by taxi.

Dawn busied herself in the kitchen making coffee. She was shocked when Ali came into the kitchen moments after the coffee finished brewing. Even more remarkable, Ali seemed awake. Ali had never been a morning person. Normally after staying up until three, she would have slept until ten or eleven. "Hey, you're up early."

"Still not as early as you I see. But yes, balancing work and school, I've gotten used to sleeping for short spurts rather than full nights. That rarely happens for me anymore, so I've adapted, but I could sure use some of that coffee," she said as a yawn overtook her.

Dawn finished doctoring one of the mugs and handed it over. "Here you go."

Ali took a sip and moaned in pleasure. "Thanks. You make the best coffee."

"One of the few things I can make in the kitchen." They grinned and stood in silence drinking the first few sips of coffee.

Ali took another long drink of her coffee. "So, are you going to tell me what's going on? I can tell something's troubling you, and I'd love to just wait and let you tell me when you're ready, but I don't have much time."

Dawn didn't deny it. She knew Ali could see it. "I would really rather not talk about it. Okay?"

"I'll relent for now and give you some time to figure out how to say what you need to. But you need to. How about we shower and I take you to breakfast?"

"Now, that sounds like a plan. You can go first. Do you remember where everything is?"

"I think so." Ali moved to the coffee pot. "I'll just take a refill for the road."

Dawn was grateful for the reprieve. She didn't want to talk about Cam, ever. Ali was the one person who could get her to if she pressed the issue. She was glad Ali was willing to give her some time, but she wondered how much. Now if she could only figure out for herself what was going on, she'd be moving in the right direction.

"Earth to Dawn?"

"Hmm?" Dawn had been lost in thought as she often was when it came to Cam. She focused on Ali, her hair wet and a towel draped around her shoulders.

"Hey, are you okay?"

Dawn shrugged. "Yeah. What's up?"

"I was just saying I borrowed your robe and letting you know the shower's free."

"Okay. Thanks." She wandered into the bathroom without another word.

❖

Cam needed to talk to Dawn and she didn't want to wait until after work to try to make things right between them. As she walked across the yard, she inhaled the sweet aroma of Dawn's flowers. It was a scent she knew she would always associate with Dawn. She rang the doorbell, but the woman who answered was definitely not Dawn. The woman was in a robe that left her sculpted legs exposed. Her shiny black hair was still wet from the shower. She obviously felt at home answering the door having just showered and with a coffee mug in her hand.

"Well, hello there." She smiled and appraised Cam from head to toe. She leaned against the doorjamb. "Can I help you?" she asked with unmistakable seduction in her voice.

Cam wondered why this woman was in Dawn's home but decided to play this out to see what happened. "Hi. I'm looking for Dawn."

"Sure. Come on in. She's just finishing in the shower. If you give me your name, I'll let her know you're here."

"It's Cam, and you are?"

"I'm Ali." She held out her hand.

Cam shook it. Then she stepped through the door but took only two steps inside trying to get a sense of the situation. She scanned the room and saw a wine bottle and two glasses on the table by the sofa, obviously left from last night. She watched as Ali moved comfortably around the house and to the bathroom and knocked on the door. Cam heard her clearly.

"Sweetie, Cam's at the door for you." She opened the door and peeked inside. A hushed conversation followed, something Cam wasn't supposed to hear. Then Ali closed the door and returned to Cam. "Dawn's just about finished in the shower. She'll be right out."

Cam felt her body tense as Ali moved fluidly through Dawn's home. She knew her way around. Who was this Ali woman that she went into Dawn's bathroom while she showered without hesitation? Dawn said she no longer dated women, and Cam had believed her, but who was this? There had to be an explanation. Cam considered leaving. She wasn't sure she wanted to hang around to find out. It was none of her business, but that didn't stop the jealously that crept in. "You know what? I'll just come back later. I didn't mean to intrude."

Cam turned to leave just as the bathroom door opened. She froze. Dawn left the bathroom with a towel wrapped around her. Cam felt her mouth go dry. From across the room, she took in the smooth alabaster skin of Dawn's body. Dawn usually had her long hair pulled back and up, but as she emerged from the bathroom, her hair was loose, and the water made it several shades darker, the deep red locks draped around her neck and shoulders flowed freely. Cam had the urge to run her fingers through Dawn's hair. Under Cam's intense scrutiny, Dawn blushed. So beautiful, Cam thought as they both stood speechless.

Finally, Dawn broke the impasse. "Cam, give me just a minute. Would you like some coffee?"

Before Cam could respond, Ali jumped in, "I'll get it."

"I'll be right back," Dawn said over her shoulder.

As Dawn turned away, her words finally penetrated Cam's clouded thoughts. "Okay," Cam replied lamely.

She wasn't alone for long. Moments later, Ali emerged with a coffee tray. "I didn't know how you like your coffee. So I left it black and brought cream and sugar."

"Thank you. Black is fine." Before Cam could ask any questions, the bedroom door opened and Dawn entered the mix.

Dawn had on jeans and a loose blouse; her hair was swept up into her usual loose bun. Cam wanted to pull it free from its restraints and let it fall around Dawn's shoulders as it had been moments before. She was sure the loose top was worn to purposely hide Dawn's sinewy figure, but it made her no less attractive to Cam.

"Ali, will you give us a few minutes please?" Dawn said. It was less a request and more a directive.

"Sure, I'll just be in the bedroom."

Dawn turned her attention to Cam. "So, you've met my sister. She surprised me last night. She flew in to see my show."

Cam's jaw dropped slightly in utter surprise. *Sister?* She tried to keep her voice from sounding accusatory. "Uh, we didn't really get that far. Your sister? Wow, you two look nothing alike."

"I know. We've spent our entire lives convincing people we have the same parents. Ali takes after our dad, and I favor our mom."

Dawn cocked her head. "Cam, who did you think Ali was?"

"I was trying really hard, apparently unsuccessfully, not to jump to conclusions."

Dawn frowned. "You can't think—"

"I didn't know what to think. But let's be fair, if you came to my door at seven in the morning and a beautiful half-dressed woman came to the door fresh from the shower, what would you think?"

Dawn ignored the question. "Why *did* you come to my door at seven in the morning?"

A number of responses flew into Cam's head. She stuck with the simple truth. "Two reasons, I wanted to thank you for all the work you did yesterday. I got in too late last night to thank you in person, but I know you're usually up early, so thank you. It looks great."

"You're welcome."

"Also, I came to apologize for the way I left things the other day. I know you're going to be busy with your show the next few days, and I leave on a business trip the day after the opening, so I wanted to put it behind us before I go. It isn't fair of me to be mad at you for your choices, as much as I disagree with them. It's your life to live the way you want."

"Thank you for saying that."

"But I wanted to get to know you better and I still do. I certainly don't want us to be at odds living next door to one another. So, can we call a truce?"

"What would this truce entail?"

The corner of Cam's mouth lifted in a lopsided grin. "I keep asking you out and you don't get upset when I don't accept your declination."

"Wait. What?"

"I'll continue to ask you out operating under the assumption someday you'll give in."

Dawn wasn't entirely comfortable with this, but she was intrigued and it didn't cut Cam out of her life. She couldn't help but smile. "It's a start. By the way," she said shifting the conversation, "when you get back, we should talk about what else you need for your yard."

"Okay."

"Now, let me formally introduce the two of you." Dawn walked over and opened the door. "You can come out now."

Ali was standing just inside the door. She had on jeans and her top was form-fitting, accentuating all her curves. Ali looked between them. "Everything okay out here?"

"Yes, no thanks to you." Dawn turned to Cam. "Cam, I would like you to meet my little sister, Ali. Ali, Cam is my next-door neighbor. I'm helping her with some landscaping."

Ali held out her hand warmly. "It's nice to meet you, Cam. I hope you didn't mind me having a little fun at your expense."

Cam shook Ali's hand, now able to laugh at the situation. "Of course not. As long as you remember I owe you one."

Ali laughed. "Oh, I like you." Without looking at Dawn, Ali asked, "Why don't you join us for breakfast?"

Cam searched Dawn's face, seeming to seek permission or give her an out.

Dawn shrugged. "Sure, why not?" Dawn glanced at Ali. "Now, I owe you one too."

❖

For Dawn's entire life, at least since she began thinking about dating, she always felt nearly invisible if Ali was also in the room. It wasn't something Ali could help and Dawn certainly didn't hold it against her. In high school, the boys and a few girls flocked to Ali. Dawn couldn't compete with her dark, exotic, and sultry sister. She didn't even attempt to. Most of the time, it hadn't bothered her. But she was sensitive to it nonetheless.

So when Cam joined her and Ali for breakfast, part of her expected the pattern to stay true. She was pleasantly surprised when Cam made her feel both seen and heard. Never once did she feel pushed to the background. Cam was friendly with Ali. She engaged her in questions about her studies and her work. She also shared stories about her, June, Kate, and Jo from when she was in college. She always included Dawn in the conversation. Ali was a natural flirt, and Dawn knew it would have been easy for Cam to reciprocate, but she didn't. Cam was respectful of both of them, but she kept it to friendly banter.

When the bill arrived, Cam insisted on paying. Ali protested. "I invited you to breakfast, I'll pay."

Cam waved her off. "No, I butted into your breakfast. I'll get it. If it makes you feel better, consider it my contribution to your education."

Ali sat back and shrugged. "That's sweet. Thank you."

Dawn joined in. "Thanks for breakfast, Cam."

"It's my pleasure," Cam said, her eyes never leaving Dawn's.

While the conversation had been friendly, the looks Cam shot her way throughout breakfast were scorching. Nobody had ever made her feel wanted over her sister. Cam definitely deserved credit for that.

Once the tab was paid, they climbed into Cam's truck and headed back to the house. Cam glanced over at Dawn who was in the front passenger seat. "Why don't we carpool to the show tomorrow? There's no reason to take two cars when we're all going to the same place. I could drive."

Dawn thought it over. "I need to be there a little early, but if you don't mind that, then sure."

"Is six early enough?"

"Yeah, that should be good."

Chapter Eight

"Dawn, relax, you'll be great. The show will be a success. Your work is amazing. You have nothing to worry about." Ali had been repeating some form of reassurance for the last hour as Dawn's nerves kicked into high gear and she tried to get ready for the show.

Dawn had two different earrings on, trying to decide which to wear. She shook her head. "I don't know why I do this to myself. Can't my work just speak for itself? Why do I have to be there?"

"Once you get there, you enjoy the interaction with the people who come to see you and your work. You get like this before every show and then end up having a great time."

Before Dawn could respond, the doorbell rang. Ali was only partially dressed. "I'll get that."

She opened the door to Cam who was decked out in a crisp dark suit with a light gray shirt and dark gray tie. Dawn's mouth went dry and her heart raced. Cam looked delicious. No way was she going there. She shook herself. Cam stood, waiting patiently, with her hands behind her back. "Come on in. It was nice of you to offer to take Ali and me to the show."

"It's my pleasure. I have something for you."

"Oh?"

"I thought about getting you roses, but I thought you would like this more." Cam brought her hands from behind her back and offered a flower pot to Dawn. "The woman at the nursery assured me these miniature Absolutely roses will do well in this climate."

"Cam, how sweet! Thank you."

"You're welcome." Cam took in Dawn's dress, letting her gaze wander lazily. She wore a simple, elegant black dress that fit her beautifully. With her heels on, she was as tall as Cam. Her hair hung loosely and Cam yearned to touch it.

Cam moved closer. "You look amazing. Stunning, actually." Cam raised her hand to Dawn's right ear and lightly touched the earring there. She was pleased when Dawn didn't back away. *Progress*. "Unless you're going for a new fashion statement, I would go with this one. It brings out the color in your eyes."

She blushed. "Oh, right. I was trying to decide on which earring when you rang the bell. I'll go take care of that. Be right back."

When Dawn walked away, Cam realized there was more, or less, to the dress than she thought. The back of the dress started at Dawn's hips, leaving her smooth back bare.

Cam escorted Dawn and Ali into the lobby of the gallery. She saw the bar in the corner. "Can I get you ladies a drink?" They both nodded and Cam headed in that direction. She returned with three glasses of white wine. Cam held her drink aloft. "I'd like to propose a toast. To an amazing artist and a successful show."

"I'll definitely drink to that," Ali said.

Dawn clinked glasses with Cam and Ali. "Thanks, you two."

Moments later, Ann, the manager of the gallery, whisked Dawn away to take care of some business.

Cam turned to Ali and held out her arm offering herself as escort. "Shall we?"

Ali wrapped her arm around Cam's. "It will be my pleasure."

They walked through the arch and into the main gallery. Many of Dawn's pieces, both large and small, were arranged along the wall. Dawn wasn't the only artist featured in the show, but she was the only one whose medium was canvas. The works of the sculptor sharing the spotlight tonight were also tastefully set throughout the room. But what captured Cam's focus was Dawn's art. "Wow."

"She's so talented," Ali said.

"I'm not sure I'll ever get used to how she takes my breath away."

Ali laid her head on Cam's shoulder. "Jesus, Cam, you say the sweetest things."

Cam said nothing.

"If my sister messes things up with you, I'm going to kick her ass. I swear if I lived closer I would fight her for you. Come to think of it, I might anyway."

"As flattering as that is I'm afraid I would have to disappoint you. I'm interested in your sister. Nobody else stands a chance."

"You have no idea how happy I am to hear you say that. Just so you know, you have my full support, but Dawn was hurt badly. She's not been willing to risk anything for a long time."

"Good to know. That means a lot. I appreciate it. Dawn needs time, and I plan to give it to her."

"Like I said, you say the sweetest things. Shall we continue?"

"Yes, let's."

Cam noticed June and Kate enter the studio and head toward her and Ali just as Dawn rejoined them. Ali wrapped Dawn in a tight embrace and whispered something in her ear. Dawn squeezed her back. Then she stepped back and turned toward Kate and June. "Hey, you two, thanks for coming."

"We wouldn't miss it," June said.

"June and Kate, I would like you to meet my sister. Ali, these are the friends we told you about at breakfast who went to college with Cam."

"It's so nice to meet you two. I've heard some great stories already," Ali said.

"It's nice to meet you too. Maybe we can all grab dinner after the show and we can get you to tell us some stories about Dawn. She doesn't talk about herself much. We'd love to hear the inside scoop."

"Now that sounds like a plan."

Dawn laughed light-heartedly. "I guess that's settled. Well then, I'll meet you all after the show. Ann tells me I must mingle, mingle, mingle."

They made their way through the show. Ali suddenly exclaimed, "Oh shit!"

They turned to look at what Ali saw. Cam saw a tall, athletic woman with short, spiky blond hair closing in on Dawn from behind. Ali turned to Cam. "Come with me. Dawn's going to need all the help she can get."

Cam didn't ask any questions. She followed Ali's lead. They moved through the crowd as quickly as possible without drawing attention. "Cam, we need to get Dawn out of the room quickly, no matter what it takes."

"Okay."

As she moved toward Dawn, Cam surveyed the scene in front of her. The woman tapped Dawn on the shoulder. Dawn turned with a pleasant smile. Even though she and Ali were still too far away to intervene, Cam saw Dawn's face turn white as the color drained from her cheeks. Her mouth drew taut and her eyes narrowed. Dawn froze and locked her gaze on the woman. She took a single step backward. Seconds too late, Ali and Cam reached Dawn. June and Kate were right behind them.

Cam reached out to put her hand on Dawn's back. Her skin was cold. "Hi, sweetheart," Cam said casually as she studied the woman who had single-handedly chilled the entire evening with her presence. "I need to borrow her. I'm sure you won't mind,"

Cam said flatly. Dawn was motionless. Cam turned to Dawn and leaned over and whispered into her ear, "Dawn."

Dawn turned toward Cam's voice and her eyes started to clear when she saw Cam. With her hand pressed to the small of Dawn's back, she guided her forward. Dawn started to move, but her steps were uncertain.

"Where are we going?" she asked.

"You and Kate are going somewhere else." Cam reluctantly handed Dawn off to Kate and waited until they were a safe distance away before turning back.

When the mystery woman tried to follow, Ali stepped in her path. Cam and June flanked Ali, each knowing only that she was on the side of anyone trying to protect Dawn. Ali spoke softly but sternly, "Lori, it's time for you to go. You're not welcome here."

Lori sneered at Ali, her fists tightened at her side. "I'm attending an art show. It was in the paper. It's a public event." She watched Kate and Dawn move across the gallery. "I came to see the artist and I'm going to talk to her."

Without taking her eyes off Lori, Ali took action. "June, will you please find a security guard? We need someone escorted off the premises."

"Certainly," June answered immediately.

"There's no need for that. I just want to talk to her." Lori's tone betrayed her intentions even if her words were innocuous.

Ali shook her head. "Not gonna happen. She didn't want to talk to you in the hospital and she doesn't want to talk to you now. She's made that quite clear. You need to leave or the next person I talk to will be the police."

Cam made sure Ali had things under control and Lori was leaving before she headed in the direction Dawn and Kate had gone. She found them in a small office at the back of the gallery. She closed and locked the door when Kate left them alone. She took the chair across from Dawn. "Can I get you anything?"

Dawn only shook her head. Cam didn't know what just happened, but a lot was going on. The shadows she'd seen so many times before clouded Dawn's face. She leaned forward and gently took Dawn's hands. "Dawn, are you okay? You're safe here."

Dawn nodded her head. "Yeah, thanks," she said quietly. She extracted her hands from Cam's and wrapped them around her owns arms to protect or warm herself, Cam couldn't decide which. They sat in silence for several minutes.

Finally, Dawn sighed. "I'm sure you have a lot of questions."

Cam removed her jacket and wrapped it around Dawn's shoulders. Dawn was vulnerable and she didn't want to push her. "No. Not now. How are you?"

Dawn burrowed into the jacket trying to get warm. Cam's scent soothed her. Her calm presence comforted her. "Her name is Lori."

Before Dawn could say anything more, there was a knock on the door. "Dawn, sweetie, are you in there?"

Cam opened the door to let Ali in, then she shut it again. Ali rushed to Dawn and wrapped her in her arms. "She's gone. Are you okay?"

Dawn stood and shook off the melancholy that enveloped her. "I'm fine. I should get back out there."

"Are you sure?" Ali asked warily. "Why don't you take a few more minutes? There's no hurry."

Dawn removed Cam's jacket and handed it back to her. "Thanks for the rescue." Then she turned to Ali. "I have a job to do. She's not going to stop me from living my life. Not anymore."

Ali squeezed Dawn's arm. "Okay. You've got a whole team close by if you need us."

"I appreciate that." Dawn walked out of the room to return to her artist duties and escape the thoughts that had flooded her mind and paralyzed her moments before.

Cam stopped Ali from following. "Ali, is Dawn in danger? Who is Lori?"

Ali was clearly confused as to why Cam didn't already know the answer to her last question. "I don't think Dawn is in any danger tonight, but this will probably bring up a lot of stuff for her. She should be the one to tell you about Lori."

"Okay."

"Cam, Dawn was—"

Cam stopped her. "It's not your story to tell. It's Dawn who needs to fill in the rest for me. When she's ready, if she ever is. She knows I'm here." When Ali clearly wanted to say more Cam shook her head. "It's okay. Let's keep an eye on her. I don't think this is over for her and she might need you."

"I think it's you she needs, Cam."

"I'll be here if and when she reaches the same conclusion."

"I know you will."

❖

Dawn stood at the edge of the main gallery and took a minute to collect her thoughts before rejoining the fray. She could handle this. Lori was gone. She had a job to do. A lot of these people had come to see her work. She couldn't disappoint them by not being fully present. She braced herself and strode back into the room.

Almost immediately, Ali was at her side. "You got this, sweetie."

"I know, but thanks for the vote of confidence."

"Sure. Oh yum, who is that?"

Dawn turned to see who Ali was drooling over. She had just enough time to whisper, "Behave." Then she welcomed the newcomer. "Robin, it's so nice to see you. This is my sister, Ali. Ali, Robin and I volunteer together at the shelter."

Ali held out her hand. "Robin, it's a pleasure to meet you." Even with everything going on, there was no way Dawn could miss the flirtatious tenor of Ali's greeting.

Robin blushed. "Nice to meet you too." She turned to Dawn. "Are you okay? I saw what happened."

"You're sweet to be worried." Dawn surveyed the room. She saw for herself that Lori was gone. Then she saw Cam across the room and she felt protected and safe. "I'll be fine."

"Okay. I just wanted to make sure," Robin said.

Ali jumped in. "Robin, since Dawn's busy with the show, how about I show you around?"

"I do need to take care of some things. I'll catch up with you later," Dawn said.

"Okay," Robin said. She and Ali walked off together.

Dawn touched base with Ann to see if she'd missed anything important while she'd been otherwise occupied. Then she wandered through chatting with each person who stopped her. During a brief pause between conversations, Cam appeared at her side and held out a glass of wine. "I thought you could use a drink."

"You're a lifesaver. Thank you."

"Any time." Dawn couldn't help but wonder if Cam was talking about the wine or the events from earlier. She decided it didn't matter. Cam had saved her in both instances.

CHAPTER NINE

Dawn gripped the shovel and dug a hole in the spot she'd selected for the new rose bush Cam brought her. Then she scooped in compost and manure from the wheelbarrow beside her to amend the soil. She was very aware Cam was in the yard next door. It sounded like she was playing with the dogs, making good use of the clear area she'd left open in her backyard. Dawn tried to block out the noises coming from Cam's yard, but the sound of Cam's sensuous voice floating over the fence touched a place deep inside her. Moments later, Dawn jumped when the voice was much closer.

"Dawn? Are you out here?" Cam stood at the gate.

Dawn took a second to settle and steady her nerves. "Yeah, come on in." She leaned the shovel against the wheelbarrow and took off her gloves to push a stray strand of hair off her forehead.

Cam swung open the gate. "Good morning. Did Ali get off okay?"

"Yeah, I dropped her at the airport an hour ago."

"I'm glad I got to meet her. She's great."

"She said almost exactly the same thing about you."

Cam moved closer. "How are you doing this morning?"

Dawn shrugged. "I'm fine. The show was great, but I always hate saying good-bye to Ali."

Cam moved closer. "I would imagine, but I meant how are you doing after seeing Lori?"

"Oh, I'm okay."

Cam gently touched Dawn's arm. "No, you're not. But if you're not ready to talk about it, I'm not going to make you. I just wanted to check on you and let you know I'm here when you're ready."

The moment Cam touched Dawn, the look in her eyes changed from grief and anguish to something Cam didn't immediately recognize, but settled on fear. Dawn broke the contact, but Cam didn't miss the change in Dawn's eyes.

Cam took a step back, giving Dawn room. "What's wrong?"

Instead of answering, Dawn asked, "How do you do that?"

"How do I do what?"

"It's like you can see inside me."

"Why does that bother you?"

"Cam, you seeing in me what others don't, doesn't bother me. It makes me feel…special."

"Then why do I see fear in your eyes every time we get close?"

Dawn looked away.

Cam moved to her. She tipped Dawn's chin up to look into her eyes again. "Don't do that, Dawn. Please don't shut me out. Why are you afraid?"

"Cam," she whispered. Cam could sense there was more so she remained silent. "Cam," this time her voice was stronger. "I feel too much with you."

"I don't understand why that's a bad thing."

"Because I don't want to feel anything at all."

Without a word, Cam put her mouth to Dawn's. There wasn't even a moment of resistance from Dawn. She pressed her mouth to Cam's, and as Cam slipped her tongue between Dawn's lips she heard a small whimper of surrender. She deepened the kiss and reveled in Dawn's responsiveness. When she raised her head, Dawn's eyes were clouded with lust and the fear was gone. "Dawn, it's a little late for that."

Cam needed another taste. She bent to recapture Dawn's mouth. When Dawn didn't resist, Cam traced Dawn's lips with her tongue, then nipped gently. Dawn moaned and her lips parted. Cam's took the opening and pushed inside. Her body was on fire. There were too many clothes between them. She slid her hand down Dawn's side and worked her hand under the hem of her shirt so she could touch her soft, silky skin.

A crashing noise right next to them pulled her out of the moment. She quickly figured out that the shovel had slid off the wheelbarrow causing the disturbance. Cam glanced at her watch. She looked at Dawn and sighed. "I wish I could stay and continue this, because that was an amazing kiss. Unfortunately, I have to go. I need to drop the pups off at Cindy and Lynn's and then head for the airport. I hope you have a great week. I'll see you on Friday. Don't miss me too much."

Dawn studied her phone, torn between answering it and letting it go to voice mail. When Cam called the first night, Dawn admitted it was good to hear from her. She had called to let Dawn know she had arrived safely and the call only lasted a few minutes, but Dawn thought about Cam the rest of the night. When Cam called the next evening, Dawn welcomed the call. By the third evening, Dawn admitted to herself she missed Cam and wanted to see her. Now, on this the fourth evening, Dawn was scared to answer the phone. Afraid she was letting Cam in too far and she wouldn't be able to go back to the way things had been when Cam returned from her trip. Dawn reached for the phone; her desire to hear Cam's voice won out over her fears of letting someone get too close. "Hello."

"Hi," Cam said, sounding surprised. "I thought I was going to get your voice mail."

"Well, lucky you. I got to the phone just in time."

"That is lucky for me."

Dawn shook her head and smiled. She couldn't help it. Cam made her feel special even from thousands of miles away. Dawn struggled with whether she should ask Cam something she'd been wondering about. "Cam, why do you keep calling?"

"Because I miss you. At the end of my day, I want to hear your voice. I want to find out how your day went and I want to share mine with you.

Dawn had no idea how to respond to Cam's open confession, so she said nothing.

Before the silence became awkward Cam spoke again, "So, how was your day? Did you do anything exciting?"

Dawn settled into the comfortable conversation. It was so easy talking to Cam when two thousand miles separated them. "It was good. I started a new painting and I'm excited about it."

"That's great. Will you tell me about it?" Cam relaxed on the bed in her hotel room. She kicked her shoes off and leaned back against the pillows propped against the headboard. She settled in to thoroughly enjoy the best part of her day. She listened as Dawn talked about her new piece. She was so passionate about her art, Cam loved listening to her.

When Dawn mentioned she liked music from the fifties and sixties, it reminded Cam about Kate's class. "Have I told you that Kate is going to be teaching a swing class?"

"No. I've always wanted to learn. That would be so much fun."

"You should definitely check it out."

"I'll think about it for sure."

"Good. What does tomorrow hold for you?"

"I have dinner plans with June and Kate."

"Oh, that should be fun for all of you. Wish I could be there."

"I'm sure your name will come up."

It felt good for Dawn to be at ease enough to joke with her. After chatting for a few more minutes, Cam heard Dawn yawn. She checked the time.

"Goodness, I had no idea how late it was. I'm going to let you go. Sweet dreams, Dawn."

"Good night, Cam."

"Thank you for picking up the phone."

"Thank you for calling. It was nice to talk to you."

Cam hung up the phone and thought about Dawn. One of those thoughts sparked her to pick her phone back up and text her friend, Jo Adams. She didn't want to call her so late if she'd already gone to bed. When she got a nearly instantaneous response, she called.

"Hey, everything okay?" Jo asked right away.

"Everything's fine. Sorry to bother you so late."

"No problem. Rhonda and I were just finishing a movie."

"How is Rhonda?"

"She's fine. We both are. Now, what's going on?"

"I have some questions I think you might be able to help me with."

"Okay. What's that?"

"My new neighbor, Dawn, has been hanging out with June, Kate, and me. She seems really comfortable with them and not so much with me. Something happened recently that made me want to ask how you got over what your dad did to you?"

"You mean how he pushed me around for years and occasionally beat the crap out of me?"

"Yeah."

"Well, it's hard to say anyone gets over it. I got through it and moved on, but I'll never really understand how someone can do that to another person."

"How did you get through it?"

"It took a while. You've got to understand, abuse of any kind messes with you. You question everything. What did I do wrong? Will I ever be good enough? Your self-esteem takes a hit. It's all part of the abuser's need to make you doubt yourself, to make you feel like you have no place else to turn."

"I'm sorry to bring all this up for you. I just didn't know who else to ask these kinds of questions."

"It's not a problem. It's a part of my past, but I did get through it. I'm glad my mom got me out of there when she did and she got herself out of the situation soon after. I'm grateful for that. Plus I had some great people around me to turn to when I needed to talk. That helped tremendously. So tell me a little more about Dawn and why you think she was in a similar situation?"

Cam summarized her interactions with Dawn and brought Jo up to speed on what happened at the art show. "I think Lori may be the reason Dawn doesn't want anything to do with romantic relationships."

"Sounds plausible."

"So, how do I get her to trust me?"

"You start with time and space. Don't pressure her. I know that's not your style, but it bears stating. If she's been hurt by someone, whether it was verbal, emotional, or physical abuse, and she managed to leave that situation, she's likely to be extremely wary of ever putting herself in that position again. It's different for everyone, so I can't give you some magic formula."

"That makes sense."

"Only Dawn can really say what might work for her. But if you can't ask her, I'd say your best bet is to back off and give her some space. That doesn't mean you can't be her friend. But lay off any romantic pursuits for now."

"For how long?"

"How important is she to you?"

"Very."

"As long as it takes."

❖

"I'm glad we were finally able to do this," Dawn said.

Kate responded for herself and June. "Us too. We're enjoying getting to know you."

"Likewise. So since you suggested Uptown, I'm guessing you've eaten here before. Do you have any recommendations?"

"Everything," June said.

A few minutes later, the waiter came and everyone made their selections, including three Cali Creamer beers from the local Mother Earth Brewery. With the lull in conversation, Dawn took the opportunity to say, "Cam said to tell you both hi."

"Oh, so you've talked to Cam while she's been away?" Kate asked.

Dawn blushed. She hadn't missed the significant look that passed between them. "Yeah, we've talked for a little while each night this week."

"That sounds serious."

"No, it's nothing like that. We're just getting to know one another better. Just like the three of us."

Neither Kate nor June said anything, but they shared a look that made Dawn start wondering. Maybe her relationship with Cam was different from what it was with June and Kate. She laughed at herself when she thought about the kisses she and Cam had shared. That was definitely different.

"So, Dawn, did I tell you I'm teaching a swing class that starts next week?" Kate asked.

"No, you hadn't, but I think Cam mentioned the class. It sounds like fun."

"You should join us. It's women, of all orientations, and I think it will be a great class. At least I'm going to try hard to make sure it is. What do you say, will you come?"

"I've always wanted to learn swing. I'm definitely thinking about it."

"Great."

CHAPTER TEN

Friday evening when Cam's plane landed, she couldn't wait to see Dawn and went directly to her house after picking up her dogs. Dawn pulled open her front door smiling. "Well, hi there, stranger."

Cam was momentarily speechless. The sight of Dawn left her breathless, and she was taken aback at her reaction. *Relax, pull it together. You can't say what you came to say if you're drooling.* "Hi, do you have a minute? There's something I need to talk to you about."

When Cam saw Dawn's slight hesitation she was confident she'd made the right decision, so she proceeded with more sureness. "It should only take a minute."

Dawn shrugged. "Okay, sure, come on in."

Cam could see the trepidation in Dawn's eyes when she tried to move closer. She stopped herself and shoved her hands in her pockets. This was why she needed to do this. "So, while I was out of town I did a lot of thinking."

"Okay," Dawn responded neutrally.

"I realize you don't trust me. You have no reason to—yet. Trust is essential to me, to trust but also to be trusted. So, until you do, until you can confide in me and know I will keep your confidences, I'm going to stop asking you out. I'm going to stop flirting. I feel like I have some pieces of the Dawn puzzle, but I don't know your story. I want to understand you and your past. I can't force you to trust me. That's something you have to decide to do. You have to believe you can share your story with me, but more than that, your hopes and dream too."

"And if that never happens?"

Cam frowned at the possibility. "I think it would be a mistake for both of us. But it's not up to me. You have to make that decision. I have to live with whatever you decide."

Dawn looked Cam directly in the eyes. "Cam, for the record, I do trust you."

Cam shook her head. "I don't think so. At any rate, not enough, not nearly enough. I hope you will one day, but we aren't there."

Dawn sensed something else between them. "Is that the only reason?"

"No. I enjoyed chatting with you over the phone this week, and I wondered if it was easier for you because I was so far away. It felt like you were freer. I liked getting to know you better."

Dawn almost nodded. *How could you tell that over the phone?*

"I want to know you better, and it's clear you're more comfortable with friendship. So, that's what I want. I want to be your friend. For now, that's all I want. I hope we can be friends because I very much enjoy your company."

"I like hanging out with you too."

"Okay then. I'm glad that's settled. I should get back to unpacking."

"Okay. See you around."

"Yes, you will."

Cam let herself out and Dawn watched her walk across her yard. Her temporary moment of relief was replaced by an overwhelming sense of loss. She was confused by her own emotions, but she didn't want to explore them too deeply.

❖

The next day, Dawn called her sister at their usual time for a video chat. After the normal pleasantries, Ali asked about Cam. Dawn filled her in on Cam's declaration.

"Are you actually okay with that?" Ali asked.

Dawn shrugged. "Sure, why wouldn't I be? I didn't want anything more than that."

"Consciously, you may have told yourself that, but it seems to me it is already past that with you and Cam. Are you forgetting I saw the way you look at her?"

"Well, it doesn't matter. I'm happy about it."

"Who are you trying to convince? Why can't you let yourself be open to the possibility of dating? It's obvious that's where she would like to see things go and you like her."

"It's not that simple."

"Yeah, it is. It is exactly that simple. You let a couple of bad experiences decide the rest of your life. You're so stubborn sometimes it makes me crazy. I know Lori hurt you, but you survived and you deserve to live a full life."

"I will not let what happened with Lori ever happen again."

"Cam isn't Lori."

"I know that."

"Do you?"

Dawn glared at her through the screen. "Yes, but it doesn't change anything for me. I won't put myself in that position again."

"Put yourself in that position? I thought you said you weren't responsible."

"I am only responsible for me, and this is something I can control."

"So, what, you're never going to trust anyone again? Never allow yourself to love anybody again?"

"I don't think I can. I'm not sure I have it in me. I can't take the risk. I don't want to."

"You don't give yourself enough credit. And I don't think you're giving Cam the credit she deserves either. Not all women are like Lori."

"It may not be fair, but it's what I have to do, to protect myself." Dawn spoke firmly, but her resolve had started to soften when she thought about Cam.

"To hide you mean. To hide behind your work and your gardens, to avoid relationships so no one can ever hurt you. The night of your art show you said you weren't going to let Lori stop you from living your life, but it seems to me that's exactly what you've done."

It stung, hearing those words from her closest ally. But what hurt more was Dawn couldn't deny that Ali was exactly right. She was hiding, afraid to face the world and the possibility of getting hurt again. She needed to live her life on her terms. She did that with her business and her painting. It was time for her to take back control of the rest of her life. Maybe it was time to truly put the past where it belonged and open up to the possibility of having someone in her life again one day.

Cam woke early and ran through a quick workout. She fed the dogs and then climbed in the shower. She felt like she had done exactly what she needed to do as far as Dawn was concerned. She hadn't lied; right now getting to know Dawn better was far more important to her than dating her. That didn't make it any easier to think about Dawn without wanting her.

The best thing to do right now was to stay busy. She climbed out of the shower and called Cindy and Lynn. She was happy to learn Lynn still had work to do on the new coop. She grabbed her keys, whistled for the dogs, and headed to the farm.

Cam let herself and the pups into the house. She stopped in the kitchen. "Good morning."

Cindy handed her the steaming mug of coffee. "Good morning yourself. How did your conversation go last night?"

Cam took a small sip. "Hmmm, thanks. It went as expected."

When it was clear Cam didn't plan to elaborate, Cindy pushed gently. "That's all I get after the way you ran out of here yesterday?"

Cam frowned at herself. "Sorry, Cin, you're right. There's plenty more to tell."

Cindy shook her head. "Listen, go on out. You and Lynn can get a start on things. I'll make breakfast and you can tell us both as little or as much of it as you want at the same time. How's that sound?"

"Good. Thanks. See you in a bit." Cam walked outside. The smells of the farm never failed to soothe her. She breathed in the freshly tilled soil, the hay hanging in bags for the goats, even the manure spread around the fields. It smelled like home. She fully relaxed for the first time in days.

Cam walked over to watch Lynn hammer a nail. Once the pounding stopped, she stepped into her sightline. "Hey, Lynn, the coop's looking good."

Lynn laid down the hammer. "It's headed in the right direction. It's nice to see you. Sorry I missed you last night."

"Yeah, sorry, I was in a bit of a hurry."

"That's what Cindy said. No worries. So, you're ready for some real work, huh?"

"You know it. Where do you want me?"

Lynn placed the next nail between two fingers and lifted her hammer. Cam effortlessly started measuring and cutting the rest of the wood based on the sheet of measurements Lynn had on the saw.

After a while, Cam stopped the saw when she noticed Cindy on the back porch. "Breakfast is ready."

Everyone sat at the table, their plates filled with pancakes, bacon, and eggs. Cam took a sip of her orange juice before beginning her story.

She filled Cindy and Lynn in.

Finally, Cindy asked, "So where do things stand?"

"We're friends. For now that's all we are. She knows I would like to explore more, but the ball is in her court."

They didn't ask Cam how she would manage being just friends when she wanted more. Cam could and had done everything she set her mind to. Lynn cleared her throat. "It sounds like you really like Dawn. How are you doing with that?"

Cam didn't have to ask what she meant. Lynn never shied away from asking the more difficult questions. "So far, I'm okay with it. When Mel died, I didn't think I would have these feelings again. It's not something I was looking for, but I know Melanie would want me to be happy so I'm not going to turn my back on the possibility."

"Well said, and I know you're right," Cindy said. "So when do we get to meet her?"

"Hard to say." Cam stood to put her plate in the sink. "Thanks for breakfast, Cin. It was delicious as always."

"You're welcome. Now you two leave your dishes. I'll take care of cleaning up so you can get back to work."

"Works for me," Cam said as she headed for the door.

Hours later, the hot sun was high in the sky. Cam and Lynn were drenched in sweat when Cindy brought out sandwiches and drinks.

"Wow. You've made fantastic progress," Cindy said as she set lunch out on the patio table.

Cam and Lynn put down their tools and took off their gloves. Cam grabbed a bottle of water. "It does look pretty good."

"It always goes much faster than even I think it will when Cam works with me. We make a good team," Lynn said.

"Yes, we do."

A couple of hours later, Lynn decided to call it a day. The new coop was done, complete with nesting boxes. She still wanted to build a chicken run and enclosed pen around the coop to protect the birds from predators, so Cam offered to return the next day.

Chapter Eleven

Dawn was nervous when she walked into the dance studio on Fifth Avenue. She had been honest when she told Kate she always wanted to learn to swing dance, but the idea of joining an all-women's class made her hesitate. Her desire to support her new friend won out over her own fears. So here she was. Her nerves dissipated a bit when she saw Kate, whose face lit with a bright smile as Dawn walked into the room. "I'm so glad you made it."

"Me too." She was a bit surprised to realize how much she meant it.

They chatted as people trickled in to the large room with a hardwood floor. When Dawn saw Cam come in, her nerves returned, but only a little. Cam was striking in her simple work clothes of slacks and a button-down shirt. Her rolled-up sleeves were her only concession to the dancing she would be doing. She smiled at Dawn as she approached her. "Hi, good to see you here."

"You too," Dawn said.

Once everyone arrived, about twenty-two women in all, Kate facilitated quick introductions. She introduced Cam and let everyone know Cam was assisting with instruction and could answer their questions as well. Then she explained that with an all female class, everyone would break into groups of those who wanted to learn to lead and people who wanted to follow. If necessary, those who wanted to learn both parts would also self identify. Once everyone sorted themselves, class began.

"Practicing the basic elements is the easiest way to learn any dance. With swing, the basic steps are walking, kick-ball-change, touch stepping, and triple stepping. Once you understand those, you can put them together to make up different styles." Kate performed a quick example of each step as she named it. "Everyone just walk in place and try each step. Just take your time and feel each of the steps as you do them. You want to dance over your feet. You don't want to lean back on your feet. You want to do each of the steps until you feel comfortable with them, and then you can start putting them together to make your own style."

Kate named, defined, and explained the steps, and the group followed her instructions. Kate observed everyone as the women copied what she did to make sure they all understood her directions. Cam also kept an eye on everyone as well. "Just get comfortable with what that rhythm feels like. Don't worry if you don't have it all down right away. Now we're going to go ahead and take those elements and put them to music. Don't hesitate to ask me or Cam if you have any questions."

Kate turned on the music and walked around her group giving guidance and knowing Cam did the same. She demonstrated each of the steps again at a slower pace making sure each woman had the basic movements down.

When Kate called for a break and everyone walked toward their bags for water, Cam made her way over to Dawn. "Having fun?"

"I am. Kate's a great teacher. It's nice of you to help out."

Cam shrugged. "Like I could say no to Kate."

Dawn laughed. "That's one of the reasons I'm here."

"Kate and I plan to grab dinner after class. Want to come?"

"Sure, sounds like fun," Dawn answered before she could think of a reason not to.

Once Kate got everyone's attention again, they started back up. "So now that you all have an idea of the basic steps, I'm going to ask Cam to join me so we can show you some of the things you can do with them. There is no expectation that any of you will be able to do any of these combinations tonight, but by the end of our six weeks, most of you will be able to do all of them or some version of them anyway."

Kate turned the music back on and Cam stepped to her. With Cam leading, she and Kate moved to the music and showed the class some simple swing dancing steps. Once the song ended, Cam and Kate broke apart and worked with the individual groups again. First Kate worked with the follow group and Cam worked with the leaders. After a while, Cam and Kate switched so that each person could try her hand at dancing.

Cam made her way down the line of women who wanted to learn how to follow, making gentle corrections and suggestions where necessary. As she got closer, Dawn became more and more nervous. Cam was her friend; she could handle this. She didn't want to embarrass either Cam or Kate, so when her turn came, she stepped into Cam's arms.

If Cam heard Dawn's sharp intake of breath, she ignored it. "Just relax and follow my lead."

Dawn met Cam's gaze evenly and moved to the music. It felt effortless. The two of them moved together smoothly. Dawn was sure she didn't get all the steps exactly right, but rather than concentrate on her feet, she focused on Cam and danced. When it ended, Dawn realized she wanted it to continue. It was over too soon.

"You two were great together," Dawn said as she, Cam, and Kate gathered their things and headed for the door.

"It's a treat to dance with Cam," Kate said.

Dawn was glad she was behind them and they couldn't see her face as she blushed and nodded silently. She shifted through the evening in her mind comparing it to a memory from her past.

The night she and Lori first met, at a party, Lori had asked her to dance. Dawn had been slightly uncomfortable, as she'd never danced with a woman, but then it had felt right; being pressed tightly against the soft curves of a woman felt delicious. Lori had made her feel wanted. Dancing with Cam tonight had inspired those same feelings, but more than that, when she danced with Cam she felt safe and protected, almost…cherished. How many other ways did Cam differ from Lori?

❖

"What are you waiting for?"

June sat on the sofa. A half-eaten pizza and several empty beer bottles sat on the coffee table between them. The two of them were in Cam's living room and the baseball game was on commercial. The dogs lay near the table ever hopeful one or both of them would send scraps their way. "Hmmm. What are you talking about?"

"With Dawn, what are you waiting for? Why haven't you asked her out again?"

Cam popped open another bottle of beer. "It's not gonna happen."

"Why on earth not?"

"A couple of reasons. For one, I took your advice and I told her I only want to be friends. So we're friends or we're working on it at least. She's more comfortable with a platonic relationship, so that's exactly what I've promised her."

"Can you actually do that?"

"I have no other choice. If I continued to pursue her romantically, I didn't have any chance of gaining her trust. I do want her friendship. Between you and me, I hope there's more to our relationship at some point in the future. But right now, friendship is all she seems capable of. So that's all I'm asking."

"If you're only friends does that mean you can date other women?"

Cam shook her head. "I've thought about it, but it doesn't feel right. I know I want something more with Dawn, and I'm willing to wait for it. It seems wrong to pursue other relationships if I'm not available, even if that's all in my own head."

"For how long? What if Dawn doesn't change her mind?"

"I'll deal with that when I have to, but for now I'm just taking it a day at a time and trying to be a good friend."

"Okay then. Shall we drink to friendship?"

Cam lifted her beer to toast. "To solid friendships."

Cam parked the bike in the garage and made her way through the house to the back door where she stopped short. Dawn was in the backyard playing with the dogs. She watched for a few moments from the door. She had never witnessed such unguarded delight from Dawn. It made her heart ache with joy. When Cam opened the back door, the dogs heard the noise and raced over to her. Dawn turned toward her with a beaming smile.

She gave Jack and Mozz full body rubs without taking her eyes off Dawn. "Hi, this is certainly a pleasant surprise."

Dawn shrugged. "I hope you don't mind. The boys were riled up and barking. I thought I'd keep them company for a little while."

Cam studied Dawn for a moment, elated to see that Dawn's guard hadn't gone back up immediately when she arrived. "I don't mind. I appreciate it and I know the boys are grateful. I didn't expect to be gone today, but I had to go into the office. So, thanks."

"My pleasure. They're great pups."

"I kinda like 'em. Listen, I don't know if you have any plans for this evening, but after I feed the boys I'm headed to have dinner with Cindy and Lynn. Would you like to join us?" Cam sensed Dawn's wariness return as she asked the question. "It's just dinner. I think you'd like them."

Dawn started to decline, not sure if her hesitation was to protect herself or if it had just become habit to deny herself. She surprised both Cam and herself when she said, "That sounds fun, but I would need to change first."

Cam's smile was brilliant. "No problem, me too. Just come back over when you're ready and we'll head out."

Dawn turned toward home and immediately doubted her decision. *I should turn right back around and tell Cam I can't go, I just remembered something I have to do. She'll know I'm lying. Besides, I want to go. From everything Cam's told me about them, Cindy and Lynn seem like great women. But it will mean being in the truck with Cam and spending hours with her. Like that is such a bad thing. Just admit that you enjoy Cam's company.*

By the time Dawn reached her bedroom, she had convinced herself that not only was she going, she was not going to go through everything she owned to pick the "perfect" outfit. She changed quickly, brushed her hair, and touched up her makeup before dabbing on a few drops of perfume. *The perfume is for me.* She didn't believe it even as she had the thought.

After feeding the dogs, Cam made another quick call. She wanted to make sure that Cindy and Lynn knew Dawn was coming as a friend. She didn't want Dawn to be embarrassed if either of them assumed something more.

By the time Dawn returned, Cam was ready. Even as her stomach clenched with desire, she said neutrally, "You smell great."

"Thank you."

Heading for the restaurant, they chatted easily about their days, but upon arriving, Dawn fell silent. Her nerves returned and she fixated on why she agreed to come. Moments after Cam introduced her to Cindy and Lynn, she started to relax. There was something about them that made her feel at ease.

"We're so sorry we couldn't make the opening of your art show," Cindy said. "We had already bought concert tickets for our anniversary. Cam said the show was amazing."

"Actually I think the word she used to describe the art was awe-inspiring," Lynn said.

"Thank you." Dawn felt her cheeks heat at the compliment. "I hope you had a nice anniversary. How long have you been together?"

Lynn reached for Cindy's hand. Cindy answered first, "Eleventeen years."

Lynn and Cam chuckled. "Eleventeen is a word Cindy made up because she doesn't remember dates or numbers," Lynn said. "It's not that they're not important, she just doesn't remember. So eleventeen is a number that means anything more than three." She looked tenderly at Cindy. "We've been together twenty-six years."

"Wow," Dawn said.

"I barely remember a time when Lynn wasn't around. But we do have pictures of Cindy at Thanksgiving and other gatherings with me and my parents that Lynn isn't in, so I know that time did exist. It feels like she's always been a part of our lives," Cam said.

Cindy chimed in. "The best part of mine."

The waitress arrived and took their drink and appetizer order.

"What are your secrets for being happy after so long?" Dawn asked.

"Well, of course there are the usual suspects: trust, communication, and growing together," Lynn said.

"But also, she's my favorite person in any room," Cindy said.

"That's so sweet." Dawn couldn't have stopped herself from looking at Cam if she'd tried. When she realized Cam was studying her, she was certain she blushed again.

Dawn had never met a same-sex couple who had been together so long. Her parents were a great model of a successful and lasting marriage, but it was different. Seeing Cindy and Lynn still so much in love after all these years gave her a sliver of hope. Clearly some people made it work.

"I can't let this opportunity pass." Dawn grinned mischievously. "You two have known Cam a very long time. What was she like as a kid?"

"Oh no," Cam groaned.

"Oh boy, where do we start?" Cindy asked.

"Let me tell you about the time she decided to bring a stray dog home and tried to keep it a secret," Lynn said.

Dawn laughed. "I can't wait to hear this."

❖

Cam pulled the truck out of the parking lot. "Did you have a good time?"

"I had a lot of fun. I really like Cindy and Lynn, and I loved hearing stories about you as a kid," Dawn said.

"Yeah, that wasn't embarrassing at all."

"Oh poor baby."

Cam froze when Dawn patted her leg. It was rare for Dawn to initiate a touch between them. It wasn't an overly intimate gesture, but she was sure it meant something. She wished she knew what. She tried to remember the thread of conversation.

"I guess it could have been worse. I'm glad you had a nice time."

"I did. Thank you for inviting me."

"You're welcome. I'm honestly a little surprised you agreed to come." Cam saw no reason to hide her confusion.

"I was too, actually. But I wanted to spend time with you."

"I'm glad." Cam was so shocked she didn't know what else to say. Dawn seemed to be relaxing around her, but she didn't want to push her luck. She enjoyed spending time with Dawn and getting to know her at whatever pace she was comfortable. However, Cam's feelings for Dawn were already surpassing friendship. She wondered how much longer she could contain them.

Chapter Twelve

Dawn didn't know why she had agreed to go dancing with June and Kate. She would be a third wheel. But when Kate had asked, she had thought it might be fun to get out of the house and out of her head for a while. Now they were on their way to Rich's and it was too late to change her mind. She decided to make the best of it, and if she wasn't having fun in an hour, she'd get a Lyft. She enjoyed hanging with Kate and June. Maybe she would have a good time.

They made their way into the club. The DJ was spinning music that inspired quite a crowd on the dance floor. They managed to snag a table halfway between the dance floor and the bar. June took their drink order and made her way to the bar. Kate grabbed Dawn's hand. "Let's dance."

On the dance floor, moving to the beat, Dawn relaxed and started to have fun. Given the pace of the music, it was comfortable to dance with her friends. But every time the DJ slowed the music, Dawn went back to the table and gave June and Kate space. She hadn't quite made her way back to the table during the latest slow song, when she saw Cam leaning against the wall nearby. Her heart rate was already high from dancing, but the sight of Cam made it race even more.

"What are you doing here? I thought you were busy tonight." Dawn hadn't meant for it to sound as accusatory as it came out, but she hadn't prepared herself for the onslaught of emotions Cam always evoked from her.

Cam quirked an eyebrow. "I was. I'm not anymore. I wanted to dance. Dance with me?"

Dawn hesitated. Things were easier between them and she'd danced with Cam at dance class many times, but there was always more space between the partners in swing dancing and she'd always had time to steel herself before she stepped into Cam's arms. This felt too unexpected, too raw. On the other hand, the song was almost over and she didn't want to be rude. "Okay."

She wrapped her arms around Cam's neck and Cam pulled her closer. They moved together seamlessly.

Dawn couldn't read the expression in Cam's eyes, but she was close enough to feel her heart racing. Her own breathing increased, and she didn't even want to try to stop herself from wrapping her arms more tightly around Cam.

As the final notes of the song played, Cam pulled away from her quickly. Then Dawn saw Lori and realized she'd pulled Cam away from her. She could only watch helplessly as Lori shoved Cam. Cam wasn't prepared. She lost her balance and fell. When Dawn saw Cam go down, her anger flared.

"Lori, what the hell are you doing?" Dawn helped Cam to her feet.

Lori glared at Cam. "She shouldn't be touching you. You're mine."

Dawn saw June and Kate standing beside her. It gave her the confidence to face Lori head on.

"She's just a friend."

"Clearly, she's more than a friend or you wouldn't be dancing to this slow ass music with her."

"It was a dance, Lori, nothing more. But I don't belong to you or anyone, and I can dance with whomever I'd like. I told you a long time ago to stay away from me. Now back off or I'm going to call the cops."

Lori stared hard at them for what seemed like a long time. Then she held up her hands. Before she backed away, she said, "This isn't over."

Cam witnessed the exchange and felt the tension. Her instinct told her to defend Dawn, but her gut told her she needed to let Dawn handle this. Dawn's words sounded calm and confident, but Cam was standing close enough that she felt her vibrating with energy. When Lori walked away, she felt Dawn release a long breath. "Why don't we get out of here?" Cam said.

They gathered their things and walked into the night. Dawn seemed lost in thought. Cam, June, and Kate stood looking at one another trying to process what had just happened. Finally, June spoke. "Does anyone want to go grab a drink somewhere quiet?"

Dawn shook her head. "I think I'd rather just go home tonight."

"We understand," Kate said.

"I can give you a ride. I'm headed home too," Cam said.

"Thank you. That would be great."

Cam led Dawn toward her truck. The drive home was quiet. Cam kept hoping Dawn would open up and tell her about Lori and their previous relationship, but Dawn stayed silent.

❖

Saturday morning, Cam had finished her usual weekend chores and wasn't interested in anything she found on television. She'd already played fetch with the dogs. It was a gorgeous summer day and she had no idea what to do with herself. Finally, she pushed off the couch. She had to get out of the house. She grabbed her keys and leather jacket and headed for her motorcycle. Maybe she'd just ride for a while and see where the road took her.

She pulled open the front door just as Dawn was about to knock and almost bowled her over with momentum. Cam instinctively reached out to grasp Dawn's hips to keep her from falling over.

"Oh!" Dawn exclaimed in surprise.

"Sorry," Cam said automatically.

Catastrophe averted, Cam and Dawn stood studying each other. Dawn was so close Cam could smell her soft scent. She released her and took a step back when what she wanted to do was pull her closer and taste her.

"Well, hi," Cam stammered awkwardly.

"Hi, are you heading out?"

"Yeah, I thought I'd go for a ride. It's such a beautiful day." Cam paused. "Wanna come?"

Dawn's eyes lit up. "I'd love to. The weather's so nice. I was coming over to see if you were up for a ride. I thought we could drive for a while and then grab lunch down at the water or something." Dawn nervously bit her lower lip. "If you want to."

Cam didn't answer right away. Her gaze was drawn to Dawn's mouth. Cam raised her eyes to Dawn's and tried to keep her voice casual. "Sounds great, let's get you a helmet."

As Cam led the way to the garage to find Dawn a helmet, Cam asked, "Is there anywhere in particular you want to ride?"

"No, I just thought it would be nice to get out of the house. And I wanted to spend time with you."

They headed north on the Pacific Coast Highway. Dawn wrapped her arms tightly around Cam and leaned her head on her back. Cam ignored the swift kick of heat she felt with Dawn so close. The ocean was on their left as she maneuvered the bike through Del Mar, Solana Beach, Encinitas, through Carlsbad, and into Oceanside. She stopped in a parking lot overlooking the ocean. Continuing any farther north would put them on the interstate. Cam enjoyed the slower pace of the scenic coastal road. They got off the bike and removed their helmets. Dawn shook out her hair and the sunlight made the red seem to burst with flame. "That was great! I didn't realize how much I miss being on a motorcycle."

"I'm glad you're enjoying it."

"I am." She clasped Cam's hand. "Let's go walk on the beach for a little while." Dawn slipped off her shoes and rolled up her jeans.

Cam pulled off her boots and set them next to Dawn's. She took Dawn's hand again. "Lead the way."

Once they were down on the beach, they headed for the water and walked along the water's edge. "Can I ask you something?" Dawn asked.

"Sure, if I can ask you a question in return."

"Okay. How did you come to live with Cindy and Lynn during high school?"

"That's a complicated story. The condensed version is that when my parents were going to be stationed in India for my dad's job with the state department, I didn't want to go. I hated the idea of leaving my friends, all the activities I was involved in, and everything familiar. My mom kept trying to convince me that it was an excellent opportunity to learn about another country and other cultures. I was having none of it. I knew what I wanted. I wanted to stay in San Diego. So then I just had to figure out a way to make that happen in a way my parents would agree with."

"And Cindy and Lynn were the answer?"

"Eventually. I didn't think of them at first. I mean I was fourteen and they didn't have any kids, so it never occurred to me. Why would they want to take on a teenager? But I was out at their farm one day, helping Lynn with something. I was doing some pretty heavy duty complaining, throwing myself one heck of a pity party because I couldn't think of a way to stay. Lynn looks at me like I'm not very bright and she said, 'So why haven't you asked us?' I didn't know what to say other than explain why I thought they wouldn't want me. Lynn studied me very carefully and then she said, 'I don't see any kids around here. All I see is a bright young woman who knows what she wants. Wouldn't hurt to have someone around for a while that can help out around the farm, once her schoolwork is done of course.' After that it all fell into place in my head. All I could think to say was, 'I could do that.'"

"Your parents simply agreed to that plan?"

"No. It took a little more convincing and a number of conversations about rules, keeping my grades up, and all that stuff. I had to wait them out, you know be patient while they got on board. But they knew once I have my mind set on something, I don't let it go easily. Cindy had been a family friend for many years and they trusted her. I'm not sure there was anyone else they would have left me with, so this was a solution that seemed to work for all of us. I'd go visit my parents for a few weeks on school breaks. Otherwise I lived with Cindy and Lynn all through high school, and their place was still my home base during college."

"That's amazing. Where are your parents now?"

"They're stationed in China. Dad keeps making noise about retiring. I'll believe that when I see it."

"It must be hard having them so far away. My parents are only in North Carolina and I miss them quite a bit."

"Sometimes, but it's easier now that we can video chat. I don't regret the choices I made. I would do it all over again because it's gotten me where I am today."

Dawn walked on silently for a few minutes thinking about what Cam had shared. Cam's younger self certainly seemed like a pretty determined person. Dawn could see that in the adult Cam as well. She would not be easily thrown off course once she'd made up her mind today either. Dawn needed to remember that. She bent down and picked up shells every now and then and inspected them. Most she dropped back down into the sand, but a few she kept in her hand. "You had a question for me."

"I do. How did you decide to become an artist? Or was it even a conscience decision?"

"It's interesting that you ask it in that way. I've loved drawing and painting since before I can remember. My parents have pictures of me at this little easel when I was five or six. I'm sure my work has improved since then, but it seems like it's always been a part of who I am. Growing up, there was never a model for living that life. There was always this voice in the back of my head that I couldn't survive with art alone. I'm not sure where that little voice came from because both of my parents were always super supportive of me and my choices.

"So even though I majored in art, I minored in business because I needed a backup plan. I worked in banking for a number of years and saved everything I could. One day I realized I hadn't painted in months. I was working so much there wasn't much time left over for my passions. So I put some thought into it and came up with a way to make a change. The idea of the T-shirt design business was a way to fund what I really wanted to do which was paint and spend time in the yard with my gardens. Making the leap from working for someone else to being my own boss was a very deliberate decision.

"Now I set my own hours. I paint when I want, occasionally design T-shirts, and blow both off if I want to spend a whole day in the yard. I call the shots. I decide when and if I want to sell my paintings. It's a pretty nice gig. But if I never sold another piece, I'd still keep painting. There are so many things, so many scenes, so much in this world that needs to be shared, which is why I sell my work. But I paint for me. I want to see those pictures on a canvas and not just in my head. Of course my studio would be much fuller if I stopped selling my work."

"True. I'd love to see those pictures of you as a kid."

"I'm sure my mom would send them if I asked, but why?"

"I like to understand who you are, what makes you you. In case you haven't figured that out."

"Oh, I've noticed."

Cam had never seen Dawn this carefree. She didn't want to do anything to scare her.

Eventually, they made their way back to the parking lot. "Are you hungry?"

Dawn nodded. "I will be soon, but why don't we head south for a little while before we stop? Maybe we can find somewhere in La Jolla for lunch."

"I know just the place," Cam said as she pulled her boots back on.

Dawn slid her shells into her jacket pocket and climbed back onto the bike and once again wrapped her arms tightly around Cam. When they stopped again, it was at a seaside restaurant in the middle of La Jolla. The hostess seated them next to a window with a view of the ocean. Aside from working in the yard, this was the most time Cam and Dawn had spent alone. It felt comfortable and easy. Dawn seemed relaxed and Cam noticed there was no hesitation between them today. Cam was hopeful.

Later, Cam parked the motorcycle in her driveway and she and Dawn dismounted. Once again, Dawn shook out her hair after she took the helmet off. Cam ached to run her fingers through it. Instead she stuffed her hands in her jacket pockets.

Dawn set the helmet on the seat. She held out her closed hand in front of Cam like she wanted to give her something. Cam took her hand out of her pocket and held it palm up.

"This is for you." Dawn placed one of the shells she'd found in Cam's palm. "To remember today."

Cam wanted to say so much more than she did. *I won't ever forget today.* Instead she said, "Thank you."

"Thank you for a great day." Dawn stood on her tiptoes and kissed Cam lightly on the cheek.

"It was my pleasure." Cam's hand tightened around the shell. She forced herself not to take more than was being offered. Her restlessness returned as Dawn walked across the yards and into her house.

The hours they spent together were easy and carefree. The lightness she felt in Dawn's presence reminded her of time with Melanie. It wasn't the same. They were two very different people. However, Cam felt at peace and comfortable with Dawn as she had with Mel. It wasn't a feeling she found very often. She stroked the shell with her thumb. She put it in her pocket and went to check on the dogs.

CHAPTER THIRTEEN

Dawn saw Cam heading into the hospital just as she headed out. It surprised her enough that she called to her. "Hey, Cam. What are you doing here?"

Cam's face lit up when she saw Dawn. "Hey, yourself. I'm here to visit some friends. How about you?"

"Visiting a friend also." Then she realized what Cam said. "Wait, did you say friends?"

Cam shrugged. "Yeah, I hang out with the kids on the oncology ward sometimes. You want to come with me?"

"I don't know."

"Up to you, but I promise, it'll be fun."

Hanging with kids who have cancer will be fun? This I have to see. "Okay, I'll come up for a few minutes."

"Great, let's go."

As she walked through the halls of the hospital with Cam, Dawn thought about backing out. But Cam seemed almost giddy with excitement, and Dawn was drawn to that.

When she entered the ward, Cam made a beeline for the nurses' station. She leaned on the counter and talked directly to the petite, black woman almost hidden by a pile of charts. "Hi, beautiful."

The nurse looked up and the face that scowled at the papers in front of her broke into a big grin. "Well hi, Cam. I didn't know you were coming today."

Cam shrugged. “I needed a dose. You know how it is.”

“Of course I do. Who’s this?” She nodded at Dawn.

“Tanya, this is my friend Dawn Oliver.”

“Nice to meet you.” Dawn offered her hand over the pile of charts.

“You too, dear.” Tanya turned back to Cam. “All right, honey, any friend of yours is cool with me.”

Cam and Dawn walked the last few feet and the automatic doors opened. Cam was quickly surrounded. It seemed to Dawn the children multiplied. It felt like absolute chaos, but Cam had a huge smile on her face. When Dawn could finally make sense of things she counted only about fifteen kids between five or six to probably seventeen.

There were a few adults in the room, parents, and nurses from the look of things, and most of them observed silently and smiled. The kids walked from their beds, some pulled IV stands, and a few came rolling over in wheelchairs. A couple of the kids had surgical masks on, apparently a precaution against germs their young bodies couldn’t fight during their current stage of treatment. One little girl with a smooth, bald head raced to Cam and threw her arms up in the air, obviously asking for Cam to pick her up. Cam easily swung her onto her hip and greeted all of them.

“Hi, everyone.” Then she studied the girl in her arms. “Daphne, are you feeling up for it?”

Daphne nodded enthusiastically. “Yes, please, let’s do it.”

Cam swung Daphne onto her shoulders and addressed the rest of the room. “Okay, places, everybody.”

Without another word, the kids and parents alike piled onto couches and chairs around a little stage. Two of the kids went to the back of the stage and began looking through a trunk. One of the older kids went over to some equipment on the side of the stage and pushed some buttons but waited for Cam before he did anything more.

Cam, with Daphne atop her shoulders, looked over at him. "Hang on a sec, Matt." Then she addressed the audience. "Hey, everyone, this is my friend Dawn. Dawn, this is everyone."

"Hi, Dawn," a chorus of voices rang out.

Dawn laughed. "Hi, everyone."

A little boy in a wheelchair spoke up, "Dawn, wanna sit with me?"

"Sure." Dawn took the last vacant seat. She was a bit confused about what was going on, but she seemed to be the only one, so she played along.

Cam exaggeratedly cleared her throat, "Heh, heh, ladies and gentleman, boys and girls, it is my pleasure to present the lovely song stylings of Daphne Gray and the Oncs."

There were hoots and hollers and loud applause. Dawn joined in wholeheartedly. Seconds later, the music started, the two kids at the back of the stage now had guitars. Cam put Daphne down and Matt handed Daphne a microphone. Cam went over to an electronic keyboard. She joined the guitarists and then all heads turned to Daphne, who danced to the music. Daphne raised the microphone to her lips and started singing. Dawn was surprised by the strong, pure voice of the little girl. She fixated on Daphne's young face, hardly able to believe the amazing sound she heard from someone so small and young.

Dawn finally looked to where Cam rocked the keyboard and her heart fluttered as she realized Cam focused on her.

The band moved effortlessly from one song into the next. But after three songs, Cam put an end to it. "Thank you all very much. Let's give Daphne and the Oncs a big hand." The applause was enthusiastic from the small audience. Daphne and her bandmates, even Cam, took their bows. Cam addressed a boy in the audience who was maybe twelve. "Ryan, are you ready to be pulverized?"

The boy Cam challenged had a mischievous glint in his eyes. "In your dreams, Cam."

Without another word, most of the kids stood and moved their chairs or rolled their wheelchairs around a large TV. Before Dawn realized what was happening, Daphne tapped her on the shoulder. She held up a book. "Dawn, would you please read this to me?"

"Of course, let's move over to the couch, so we can be more comfortable. By the way, I loved your singing. You have a beautiful voice."

"Thanks, I love singing. Whenever Cam comes and I'm feeling good enough we put on a show."

"How long has Cam been coming to visit?"

Daphne cocked her head in thought. "Well, as long as I've been coming, and I've been getting treatments for about two and a half years. She used to hang out with us while Melanie was getting treatments, and then after…well, she just kept coming. We always have so much fun with her."

"How old are you, Daphne?"

"Nine."

Dawn couldn't believe this girl was only nine. She was so confident and articulate. But she was also small for her age. As she and Daphne settled on the couch, Dawn saw Cam engaged in a video game battle with Ryan. Daphne climbed into Dawn's lap as she opened the book and began to read aloud.

Cam was aware of where Dawn was and what she was doing. She watched her for a while, losing focus on her game. Ryan's cry drew her attention back. "Ha, gotcha!"

"Not for long, my friend, not for long," Cam replied enthusiastically. The battle waged on, Cam refocused and became engrossed in combat.

Dawn and Daphne moved from reading to playing dolls, where a couple of other kids went to play with them. Cam glanced over again when Ryan rose from the soft chair in front of the TV, in defeat. His seat was quickly taken by one of the older kids, ready to challenge Cam. She turned back to the game.

This process was repeated over and over as each challenger went down in flames.

Finally, Cam told Dan, who was next in line that she would take him on next time she visited. Dawn helped Daphne and the other kids clean up the toys. Daphne hugged Dawn and asked her to return soon. Without any discussion, Cam and Dawn walked out of the ward together.

They walked for a while in silence. Cam's hands were in her pockets so she wouldn't be tempted to reach out to Dawn, the connection she felt for her already so tangible.

She glanced at Dawn. "So?"

"So…?"

"Did you have fun?"

"Yeah, I did. I was skeptical. It's not a place you expect to have fun."

"I'm glad you had a good time."

"I did. Thank you for sharing that with me. The kids are great. Some of them seem so much more mature than their age."

"All of them are great. The group changes a bit from visit to visit, since different kids come in for treatments, some kids get better, and some kids, well, they aren't so lucky. Each one has been through a lot. It makes them grow up fast. But I like to think I can help them have a little fun. It can be such a dreary place, you know?" Cam shrugged self-consciously and shook her head.

"You showed no mercy while playing video games with them. All the kids liked that; it was obvious. You don't treat them any differently just because they're sick. I imagine most of them don't get that many places."

Cam shrugged again. There was no way she could explain everything she felt or thought when she was with them, but she was comforted by Dawn's understanding. "They're just kids."

Dawn caught the tone in Cam's voice. *Not to you. Every one of them is special to you. How much does it cost you when you lose one?* "I understand more than you might think."

"What do you mean?"

"I volunteer at a shelter for women and children who are victims of domestic violence."

"I didn't know that."

"It's not something I talk about very often. I help them with their garden and sometimes teach basic gardening skills to some of the women. But what gets me the most is the kids. They've been through so much in their lives, but time and again they bounce back. They're so resilient. That's not to say they don't have their own struggles, but it's almost as if they know they're safe at the shelter…a lot of them seem carefree and happy. That helps their moms realize they made the right decision to leave."

"I can only imagine that is very rewarding work," Cam said.

"It is. I enjoy it very much."

"What made you decide to give your time there?"

Dawn studied Cam's face trying to discern what Cam was really asking. All she saw was genuine curiosity.

"That is a story for another day."

"Fair enough."

Cam sat in her backyard with June and Kate. It was the anniversary of Melanie's passing. She was melancholy, and they didn't want her to be alone. The three of them sat around the fire pit and drank wine and swapped stories and memories of Melanie. They did this each year, a memorial of the life Melanie lived. Cam was a little beyond tipsy and she didn't care. She hurt and wanted the pain to go away.

As the light waned, June stood. "We should go. Will you be okay?"

Cam nodded. "Sure, I'm just gonna sit and watch the fire for a while, then I'll head inside."

They said their good-byes, and Cam poured the last of the wine. On a night like this, she had no desire to climb into bed. It reminded her in stark detail Melanie was gone and she was all alone. The tears started, and she didn't try to stop them, letting them soothe her pain.

Dawn stepped outside to take in the stars and fresh night air. She smelled the smoke. She didn't hear the voices she expected over the fence, so she walked over to make sure the fire was contained. She stopped when she saw Cam sitting all alone. Cam must have sensed the movement because she met Dawn's gaze. "Hi," Cam said quietly.

The torment in Cam's dark eyes wrenched Dawn's heart. "Hey." Dawn moved farther into the yard. "Are you okay?"

Cam shook her head. "I'll be fine."

Dawn didn't miss the slight slurring of Cam's words.

Standing directly in front of Cam, Dawn held out her hand. "Let me help you inside."

"No. I don't want to go to bed. I miss Melanie."

"You don't have to go to bed. But you shouldn't stay out here all night."

When Cam stood, she wobbled and had to grab Dawn to keep from tipping over. Dawn was ready for that and took on her weight. She shifted so her arm was around Cam's waist. She helped Cam inside and to the couch. When Dawn tried to steer Cam onto it, she tipped over and both of them landed on the couch, Cam slightly on top of Dawn. "Sorry," Cam said flatly. She tried to scoot over. She didn't make it far; moving on the soft couch in her condition was difficult. She managed to look into Dawn's eyes. "Please stay."

Dawn searched Cam's pain-filled eyes, wondering what this was all about, but at that moment she couldn't deny Cam's request. "Okay, for a little while."

Cam laid her head on Dawn's lap and closed her eyes. Dawn sought only to soothe as she brushed Cam's hair off her forehead.

Soon she heard the change in Cam's breathing and realized she had fallen asleep. She sat watching Cam for a while, losing track of time. The pain vanished from Cam's features during slumber. As Dawn studied Cam and listened to her breathe, her heart fluttered and her resolve began to soften.

❖

Cam smelled coffee. Her eyes fluttered open. It took her a minute to get her bearings. When she realized she was on her couch, fully clothed, the events of last night gradually came back to her. *Dawn!* She groaned inwardly. She had fallen asleep on Dawn crying about Melanie. She covered her head with a throw pillow. *Great.* She lifted herself up and half expected to see Dawn standing in the kitchen. She was both disappointed and relieved she wasn't there.

She rubbed her face with her hands trying to clear the cobwebs from her memory of last night. She needed to apologize to Dawn, but it should probably wait until her stomach wasn't threatening to revolt and her head cleared. She pushed off the couch and headed for the bathroom in search of something that would dull her throbbing head. She was grateful it was Saturday and there was nothing she had to do.

❖

Dawn strolled along the water's edge. She often came to watch the ocean when she had serious thinking to do. She hadn't slept. She'd sat listening to Cam's breathing and contemplated the promises she'd made to herself. Were they worth it? Was she giving up on life? Had Ali been right? Even after she left her in the early morning hours, she was still too stirred up to rest. Now, as the sun rose over the water, she thought about Cam.

The devastation she saw in Cam's eyes the previous evening struck a chord deep inside her. What she had to figure out now was what to do about her. Cam had been clear she would like them to be more than friends. As Dawn kept her vigil throughout the night, she finally admitted to herself she was tempted by the possibility.

Dawn couldn't believe how she thought for one minute that Cam was anything like Lori. Aside from a very slight physical resemblance as far as their build, there was virtually nothing similar about them. Cam was strong yet tender, patient, compassionate, and kind. Lori was none of those things. Oh, she played a good game for a while, just long enough for Dawn to fall for her fake charms. Gradually, Lori revealed her true self. Cam lived her life with honesty. There was never any pretense with her.

Cam was surrounded by lifelong friends which, in and of itself, should have been a testament to her character. Lori had worked hard to isolate Dawn while they were together even bad-mouthing her sister and parents at every opportunity. Cam visited sick children in the hospital and helped her neighbors. There really was no comparing the two. They were completely different women. She had to stop judging Cam on a surface level. She had to examine the whole situation. Maybe Cam was worth the risk.

Late Sunday afternoon, Cam knocked on Dawn's front door. Dawn answered with a tentative smile. "Hi."

Cam grinned sheepishly. "Hi, can I interest you in a walk?"

"Yeah, that sounds nice." They walked down the porch steps and took a right on the sidewalk.

Cam glanced over at Dawn. "I want to apologize for Friday night and thank you for taking care of me."

Dawn shook her head. "You don't need to apologize or thank me. That's what friends are for."

"It was still very sweet and I appreciate it."

"Well, then, you're welcome." They shared an easy smile and kept walking. "Can I ask you a question?"

"You can ask me anything."

"Who's Melanie?"

"You don't mess around do you? You could have started with an easy one," Cam said wryly.

"I'm sorry. If it's too personal you don't have to answer."

"It is personal and I do have to answer, because you need to know. I probably should have told you before now, but when's the right time to share something like this?"

Dawn didn't say anything, giving Cam the time she needed to continue.

"Melanie was my lover. We met about seven years ago. It was one of those chance encounters, totally random, in a grocery store of all places. I was at the meat counter getting steaks for a cookout. I already had the beer in the cart. I caught Melanie out of the corner of my eye. She was this leggy brunette smiling at me like she knew me. Somehow she struck up a conversation right there on the spot. I have no idea what we talked about. I can only imagine it had something to do with the cookout. Anyway, you don't need all these details. To make a long story short, I invited her to the cookout. She followed me home and helped me prep for it. One thing led to another, and soon we were dating and in love. We had an amazing relationship and four years together."

Cam cleared her throat and looked directly at Dawn. "Then she got sick." She stared straight ahead as she explained the rest. "Cancer. She was young, strong, and healthy. All the doctors thought she would beat it. But after almost a year of battling, she lost her fight. She's been gone two years this past Friday."

Dawn laid her hand on Cam's. "Cam, I'm so sorry. You must miss her terribly."

"Sometimes it still hurts. I was so in love with her. A part of me will always love her." Cam turned her hand over and linked her fingers with Dawn's. "But I'm still here and very much alive. I made a promise to Melanie before she died that I wouldn't close myself off to the possibility of finding love or that passion with someone else. It hasn't mattered before now because there hasn't been anyone I thought I might find that with. There wasn't anyone else that mattered, until I met you."

"Cam..." Dawn stared down at their linked hands. She had no idea how to respond. She could see the truth in Cam's eyes, she could see the passion she felt for her, and it concerned her, but not as much as it once did.

Cam squeezed Dawn's hand lightly and let it go. "Well, that's enough of the heavy stuff for today. How about we talk about what else we can do in my yard?"

Cam looked vulnerable, but Dawn was hesitant. Flowers and plants seemed like a safe topic. "Sure. I've wanted to talk about what trees we might put back there." Dawn was glad Cam had cut her off. She wasn't at all sure she was ready to share what she'd almost said.

Chapter Fourteen

The following Saturday, Dawn weeded the flowers she planted weeks before in Cam's backyard. Most of the choices she made for Cam's yard required little maintenance, easier for someone not used to gardening. But she couldn't resist putting in this splash of color.

The sun beat down, but a light breeze made it bearable and rock music played softly in the background. The dogs lounged in the shade of the big maple tree. Dawn sat back on her heels and wiped her brow with her sleeve. She glanced over to where Cam was digging a large hole to plant another tree on the side of the yard they hadn't filled in yet. The sun glinted off her sweat-slicked hair. The simple scene knocked the breath out of her. It felt so peaceful and so right. *I'm falling in love with Cam.* As Dawn had the thought, her first instinct was to run and hide. She checked that impulse and studied Cam. *Cam has been steady and patient, never asking for anything more than I can give. Still, somewhere along the way I started to fall in love with her. Cam would never believe me if I told her. She has absolutely no reason to. I'm ready. She's waited long enough, too long.* She braced herself and dove in. "Cam?"

"Hmm?"

"Can we take a break?"

Cam leaned her shovel against the fence. “Sure. Let’s get out of the sun and get something cold to drink.”

Dawn stood up and dusted herself off.

Jack and Mozz must have sensed something happening. Both raised their heads, watched for a moment, and ambled after them.

“What can I get you to drink? Water, lemonade, iced tea?”

“Ice water please.”

“I’ll be right back.”

Cam let herself into the house to get their drinks. The dogs both took long drinks from their water bowls and plopped down on the covered patio. Dawn tried to sit, to relax, but too much swirled around in her head. She couldn’t settle down. Instead she paced the patio anxiously.

Cam held out the water. “Here you go.”

“Thanks.” Dawn took a long drink and then set it on the table.

Cam sat in one of the patio chairs around the table.

“Sorry, this is hard. Give me a minute, okay?” Dawn said.

“Take all the time you need.”

See, damn it. It’s when you say sweet things like that that just makes me want to curl up on your lap and snuggle in forever. And that scares me more than you could ever know.

Dawn didn’t know where to begin. This was not a story she had told often. In fact, only her family knew the whole story. But they already knew the background and players. She decided the best thing to do was start at the beginning.

“I was what most people would call a late bloomer. I didn’t date much in high school. The boys were much more interested in dating Ali, and it didn’t matter much to me. It never occurred to me that was because I was going to be more attracted to women. We lived in this tiny town in North Carolina, and that wasn’t something anyone talked about.

"Anyway, my senior year in high school, I met Kevin and we hit it off. I realize now we should have just stayed friends, but it was the deepest connection I'd ever had with a guy. At the end of the school year, he asked me to marry him and I said yes. We were both headed out here to college, and at eighteen it made perfect sense. We got married by the local justice of the peace just before we left for school. We were young and stupid and convinced our connection was love.

"It didn't last long. Ironically, two months after we got to college, Kevin realized he was gay. When he told me, I was devastated. But not for the reasons you might think. Strangely, it didn't matter that he liked men and didn't want to be married to me anymore. I was okay losing a husband, but I was distraught over losing my best friend.

"It turned out he felt the same way. So we got divorced and moved into a two-bedroom apartment together. I kept his last name because I liked it better than my birth name, but aside from that we remained great friends. He dated men and so did I."

Dawn paused to take a few sips of water. "Anyway, because of that whole situation, I realized I liked being friends with guys. Men are so…uncomplicated. Once we graduated, Kevin followed his dream and went to San Francisco. I moved in with Peter, who is straight but we never dated. I got a job at a bank." Dawn shrugged. "It was something to do while I figured out what I wanted to do with my life. Not a lot of positions right out of college for someone with a fine arts degree."

Cam noticed the first hints of the shadow in Dawn's eyes.

"One of the girls at the bank invited me to a party one weekend. I didn't have any other plans and it sounded like fun, so I went. The music was good and the drinks were strong. I was standing off to the side of the dance floor wishing I knew more people there, so I wouldn't feel self-conscious dancing. All of the sudden, this woman came up to me and took the drink out of my hand and set it aside. Her eyes sparkled with laughter and she said, 'Let's dance.' I had danced with women in groups of people before, so at first I thought nothing of it. We danced and I enjoyed more than the music.

"When a slow song started playing, I turned to leave the dance floor. She stopped me and said, 'What's your hurry?' She pulled me to her. At first, I froze. I'd never danced like that with a woman before. But then…then I couldn't figure out why I never had. It felt so right. We danced for hours. I kept looking forward to the slow songs, so I could hold her again and be held by her. Then toward the end of the night, she pulled me over to a corner and she very softly, very sweetly kissed me. She was nice and patient with me as I figured everything out. It was all so new for me."

It wasn't easy for Cam to remain silent. It was difficult for her to listen to Dawn talk about being in another woman's arms. But Cam knew how long it had taken Dawn to trust her and she wasn't going to risk doing anything to mess that up now. "I had never felt like that, ever. The rest of it all happened so naturally. Lori and I started dating, and after a few months she moved in with me and Peter. I was in heaven. I had never been happier in my life. But shortly after she moved in things started to change. At first it was a cutting comment about my appearance or lack of skills at something when nobody was around. She would always say she was joking or play it off in some way. She claimed I should have a thicker skin. My self-esteem plummeted, but of course I was too close to the situation to recognize what was happening."

Cam was fully aware of the haunted look that now gripped Dawn's features, certain the other shoe was about to drop.

"It escalated. The first time she hit me, she said it was an accident. I know it sounds so clichéd now, but she really seemed deeply sorry. She pampered me for weeks afterward. Then the cycle began. I'm sure you know it. I couldn't convince myself that it was bad enough to leave. One day, after Lori and I had been dating a little over fifteen months, I got off work earlier than expected. When I got there, I couldn't find Lori or Peter. Then I did. They were together in Peter's bed."

Dawn's voice, hollow with emotion, gripped at Cam's heart. Still, she did nothing. Her only reaction was the clenching of her fists as she felt Dawn's pain like it was her own. Dawn needed to get this out.

"I stumbled backward trying to get away from what I saw. That's when Lori finally noticed I was there. I ran to my room and locked the door. I had no idea what to do next. My world was shattered. Lori had never even been with a guy, and Peter was my best friend. I felt beyond betrayed, like my insides had been ripped out. Lori and Peter apologized through the door. They swore it was the first time it had happened, blamed it on too much alcohol from a drinking game. I have no idea if any of that is true and it didn't matter. After a while, I stopped listening. I couldn't stand it anymore. I turned on the stereo to drown out their voices. Finally, I had a reason to leave. She cheated on me. Nobody had to know the rest.

"Still, I felt lost and alone. There was only one place I could think to go. So, I packed a few clothes and the things that were important to me and headed for Ali's. I got as far as the stairs… that's where things get confusing. I was at the top of the stairs… suddenly, Lori was there and she grabbed my arm, I think. I don't know. I honestly don't. I don't know whether I pulled away from her and slipped or whether she pushed me, but whatever the cause, I fell down the stairs. I woke up two days later in the hospital with a concussion, a broken leg, and lots of bumps and bruises. I was lucky it wasn't worse. My parents and Ali were there, but so was Lori.

"My family didn't know what had happened and assumed I'd want her there. I didn't want to look at her. As soon as she left the room, I told them I didn't want her there and my dad made her leave. She wasn't family and she had no legal standing as my 'girlfriend.' The hospital wouldn't let her in to see me after that. When I explained what had happened, Dad and Ali went to get my things. Lori gave them an earful of apologies and kept saying my fall was an accident. She tried to convince them that if she could just talk to me we could sort it all out. They told her it would be up to me if and when I reached out and that she should let me be. Once I was well enough to travel, I flew back to my parents' farm to recuperate. Lori tried to get in touch with me for days. She left voice mails. She even called Ali. Luckily, she didn't have my parents' number and nobody told her that's where I was. All of her messages were more of the same. 'I made a mistake. It will never happen again. Please forgive me.' All the things she'd said before. This time I was strong enough or removed enough from the situation to see the truth. Eventually, I had enough and finally responded. I sent her an email that said, 'I don't ever want to talk to you again. Leave me alone.'

"I blamed myself for a long time. What did I do wrong? Why didn't I see it coming? What if I had been better? My self-esteem was gone. I know that is what they do. They break you down. They isolate you. Hell, we lived with Peter and he didn't know what was happening. She hid it that well. I know it wasn't my fault, but...sometimes I still wonder what I could have done differently."

Cam reached out to put her hands on Dawn's, which were ice cold. She waited until Dawn lifted her eyes. "I'm sorry that happened to you."

Dawn wasn't sure what reaction she'd been expecting, but this quiet comfort touched her more than she anticipated.

"I'm sure telling me all that was exhausting. Do you need anything?"

"That's really sweet, but I think if we can just sit here for a little while and enjoy the yard and the weather, I'd really like that."

"You got it."

Dawn wasn't sure how long they sat there, but the silence was comfortable and easy. Cam seemed content to simply sit with her and enjoy the day. Eventually, Dawn said, "I guess we should get back to the yard."

"Never mind about that," Cam said. "You've had a hard day. Let me walk you home and I'll finish this yard work tomorrow. You can help then if you want."

Dawn nodded. She was exhausted from recounting the pain of her past. "I don't even know why I waited so long to tell you. It's not like what you had to go through with Melanie."

"No, it's not. She didn't choose to betray or hurt me. You were lied to, abused, and cheated on. It wasn't easy to lose Mel, but I know it wasn't her fault. You don't have to apologize for not telling me your story sooner. You told me when you were comfortable. I see it still hurts you." Cam made sure Dawn got safely inside. "I'll be home all day if you need anything."

"Thanks. I think I'm just going to shower and lie down for a while."

"Okay."

❖

When Dawn stepped from the shower and towel-dried her hair, she realized she wouldn't be able to sleep. Still in her bathrobe, she poured a glass of lemonade and went into the backyard hoping the serenity of her gardens would help her regain balance. The sun was sinking quickly; it would be dark soon. Dawn had heard Cam work out before and recognized the sounds. But something was different this time. The cadence was off. Curious, she made her way through her gate and into Cam's yard.

She tried to get Cam's attention by calling her name. She could tell something was wrong. Cam was attacking the heavy bag. She pummeled the bag like she fought for her life. Dawn knew to the core of her being that Cam would never intentionally hurt her, but she was afraid if she touched Cam she might get a fist in the gut for it. She moved into Cam's line of sight.

Cam stopped punching the bag, breathing hard, and drenched in sweat. "Hey. What's wrong?"

"That's what I was coming to ask you. Who were you trying to kill just now?"

She shrugged. "Lori mostly since I had a face to focus on, but also Peter."

Dawn was touched beyond words. Without thinking, she moved close to Cam and took her hands. When Cam flinched, she looked down. She rubbed her thumbs over Cam's red knuckles. She just stopped herself before bringing them to her lips. "Thank you." She reached up and laid her hand against Cam's flushed cheek. "I'm not looking for a white knight or a protector. I'm not looking for someone to kill them, but it means a lot that you want to. Let's go get some ice on these hands."

As she entered the kitchen, Dawn crossed to the freezer and took out the ice bucket. She indicated the stools at the bar. "Come sit over here." Dawn searched through drawers until she found the kitchen towels. She took out four. In two she placed enough ice to cover Cam's knuckles. She carried it all over and wrapped each of the ice-filled towels around Cam's injured hands.

Dawn mumbled "sorry" when Cam winced. She secured the icepacks to Cam's hands with the extra towels. Dawn had been so engaged in her immediate task that only at that moment did she realize how she and Cam were both dressed. Cam had taken her shirt off at some point and sat in her shorts and sports bra. She stared at Cam's bare midriff, slick with sweat, and peered down at her own robe knowing there was nothing underneath. Blood rushed to her cheeks. Her first aid ministrations put her between Cam's legs. *Too close.*

She knew she should back away, but couldn't make her feet work. She didn't want to move. She had wanted Cam for months.

She didn't want to over analyze it anymore. She was tired of denying it, she just wanted…Her gaze wandered up Cam's nearly naked body, over the strong thighs and lean hips, over the flushed skin of her torso, up her small tight breasts, the nipples stiff peaks straining against the sports bra, to the rapid pulsing of her neck. When her eyes finally landed on Cam's, she fell into the deep blue pools of lust and longing.

"Dawn?" Cam's voice was hoarse, ragged, and tight.

"Hmm?" Dawn was having trouble maintaining a coherent thought she was so distracted by the wash of desire pulsing through her.

"You need to leave."

Dawn winced, stung by Cam's words. "What? Why?"

Cam licked her lips that had gone dry as Dawn focused on them. "Because if you don't, I'm afraid I might break a promise I made to you."

Dawn met Cam's tortured gaze steadily. "What if that's exactly what I want you to do?"

Cam swallowed hard. "Then you better tell me right now."

"How about I show you?" Dawn bent her head and claimed Cam's lips with her own.

There was nothing gentle about the kiss. It was hungry and demanding, and Cam was overcome with the arousal that flooded through her. It took a second to realize this was happening. Her brain kicked in just long enough for her to realize actually touching Dawn was infinitely better than any of the many fantasies she had concocted over the past few months. She needed to get in the game. She shook the towels off her hands, paying no attention as ice scattered all over the floor. With her hands now free, she plunged them into Dawn's hair and let the soft, lush feel of her flaming red locks center her.

Cam wanted to go slow and gentle to show Dawn she was cherished, but they were past that point. The lust she saw in Dawn's eyes almost sent her over the edge all by itself. She slid her hands down Dawn's back and settled on her hips. She gently pushed her back a step, never breaking the kiss. The space gave her room to slide off the stool. She pulled the tie of Dawn's robe free and moved her hands to the smooth, alabaster skin of Dawn's hips once more before sliding to cup her beautifully tight ass. She hitched Dawn up into her arms where Dawn's leg automatically wrapped around Cam's hips.

The pressure this caused on Dawn's pulsing center as it connected with Cam's naked stomach made Dawn moan in pleasure. She broke the kiss long enough to look into Cam's eyes. She saw the desire and heat she expected but there was more. There was wariness, worry, and uncertainty. She had never seen anything like it in Cam's eyes before, and she was sorry to see it now. "Please." Dawn had to clear her throat it was so tight with need. "Please, Cam, take me to bed. I need to feel you."

The uncertainty fled from Cam's eyes and Dawn almost cried out in joy. A steely determination now glinted in Cam's eyes as she walked them to the bedroom, Dawn still in her arms. When they reached the side of the bed, Cam gently set Dawn on her feet. Then she pushed the robe off her shoulders and let it pool on the floor at their feet.

Sensing Cam's hesitation, Dawn took things into her own hands. She freed Cam's breast from the sports bra and took a nipple into her mouth. Cam gasped at the contact and her hips thrust forward automatically seeking more of Dawn's touch. Dawn licked and sucked Cam's tight, hard nipples. She managed to spin Cam around and tugged off her shorts before pushing her back onto the bed. She followed, climbing on top of Cam.

As their naked bodies made full contact, both of them moaned. Dawn took advantage of their position and kissed Cam fiercely. With her leg between Cam's thighs, she felt the heat and wetness at her center. Dawn thrilled as Cam opened herself, holding nothing back. She wasted no time, shifting slightly so her hand had free access and slid it down Cam's glistening torso over her tight abs, into the dark curls at the base of her stomach, through the slick folds, and she thrust two fingers deep inside. Cam bucked her hips in shocked pleasure and her mouth opened with a strangled, "Oh my God!"

Dawn pulled her fingers almost out and plunged them in again. Dawn stroked Cam's clit with her thumb while she buried her fingers deeper with each thrust. It only took moments before Cam's entire body tensed and her pleasure exploded, coating Dawn's hand. Her body bent in two and she cried out, "Yes, Dawn, yes." Cam sank back on the bed, completely spent. Dawn left her fingers inside until Cam's body finished pulsing around them.

Then she slowly slipped them out and kissed Cam's cheek, forehead, and closed eyes, before placing her lips to Cam's mouth. Cam groaned and opened her mouth to give Dawn access. It was a tender kiss, a wonderful but stark contrast to the frantic lovemaking of moments before. Dawn ended the kiss, shifted, and laid her head on Cam's shoulder. She flung her leg over Cam's and snuggled in. She smiled when Cam's arms came around her, keeping her close. She had no words to describe how she was feeling. All she could do was hold on. She closed her eyes and listened as Cam's breathing slowed and she drifted off to sleep.

Chapter Fifteen

Cam's eyes flew open. She was instantly fully awake. Her body was on fire. All she could see was a curtain of red hair as Dawn was bent over her torso paying special attention to her breasts. Her clit throbbed as she felt Dawn's fingers languidly stroking her center. She hissed in air and expelled it forcefully. "Jesus, Dawn."

Dawn glanced up and met her eyes, the hunger in her eyes was almost Cam's undoing. With a lustful smile, Dawn moved down Cam's body and took her slick, wet folds into her mouth. Cam bucked her hips and she came instantly. Dawn licked and sucked while she slid two fingers inside Cam. Her body writhed and she flailed her arms trying to find something to hold on to as pleasure tore through her. Cam gripped the sheet as her body raced to another orgasm. "Fuuuuuck!"

Dawn tenderly kissed her way back up Cam's body as it settled. She laid her full weight on top of Cam and sucked Cam's bottom lip into her own. She lifted her head to meet Cam's eyes. "Good morning."

"Yes, it is," Cam said, satiation lacing every word.

Cam slid her hands into Dawn's hair pushing it back from her face and pulled her down for a long, hot kiss. Dawn shifted so she was straddling Cam's leg. As she pressed against her thigh, Cam felt the wet heat of Dawn's arousal. She lifted her thigh increasing the pressure and thrilled at Dawn's moan of pleasure. Just as quickly, she lowered her leg, and as Dawn was gasping at the loss of contact, she moved her hand between them to cup Dawn's center. Dawn ground into her. Dawn held on to Cam's shoulders. "Fuck me. Fuck me, Cam. I need to feel you inside me."

Cam moved her fingers that had been stroking Dawn and drove them inside her. Dawn automatically adjusted so she could take Cam in farther and her hips thrust up and down as Cam pushed and pulled, in and out, in and out. When Dawn's body went rigid as she gathered on the edge, Cam pumped into her once, twice, three more times, and she fell off the cliff. The orgasm ripped through her, and all she could do was hold on to Cam until it subsided. Then she collapsed in a satisfied heap burrowing her face into Cam's shoulder. Cam lazily stroked Dawn's back.

When Dawn finally opened her eyes, she had a clear view of Cam's neck. She leaned forward and kissed it. "Thank you."

The soft rumble of Cam's chuckle shook her whole body. "Any time, seriously."

They lay in silence for a few moments before Cam spoke again. "I can practically hear you thinking."

Dawn lifted her head to see Cam clearly but didn't say anything.

"Do me a favor, let's enjoy this morning. We can figure out what this means after a shower. Care to join me?"

"I thought you'd never ask."

Cam slipped from the bed and headed to the bathroom. Dawn followed closely behind her. Cam twisted on the water and turned to take Dawn in her arms. She kissed her while the water heated. She maneuvered them into the shower and let the water cascade over them. Cam slid her hand down Dawn's side, and she skimmed her fingers on the underside of her breast. Then she ran her thumb over the taut nipple and swallowed Dawn's moan. She moved her mouth from Dawn's lips and worked her way down her neck to the swell of her breast and raked her teeth across her nipple.

Dawn gripped Cam's shoulders and her knees threatened to buckle. Cam gave the other nipple equal attention before licking her way down Dawn's stomach. She knelt in front of her and spread her wet lips before dipping her head and taking her clit into her mouth. Dawn dug her nails into Cam's shoulders as she struggled to stay upright. Dawn reached a hand around to grasp Cam's hair and keep her close. Cam held Dawn's hips tightly, holding her up. She licked and sucked until Dawn's body reached the peak and she crashed over the other side. The force of the orgasm bent Dawn in half, and if Cam hadn't been there to catch her, she would have fallen. Cam stood and held Dawn closely. As her body settled, Cam kissed her. Then she took the shampoo off the shelf and lathered her hands with it before plunging them into Dawn's hair. "You have no idea how long I've wanted to get my hands in your hair."

"Probably as long as I've wanted to do this." Dawn grabbed Cam's firm, wet ass and squeezed.

Cam's laughter echoed off the shower walls. "Probably."

"How about I make us some breakfast and we can talk?" Cam asked as she rubbed her hair dry.

"Sounds good. I'm just going to run over and put some clothes on. I would just put the robe back on, but I've seen what it does to your concentration."

"Ha ha. You can't blame me, can you?"

"Hey, I'm not complaining."

"Thank goodness and you're okay about last night?"

"Oh, I'm more than okay. Do you have any regrets?"

"The only regret I would have is if what happened last night was too much too soon. If it meant we couldn't ever be together again."

"Rest assured. I definitely want more of what we did last night."

"Okay. Then go get dressed and I'll make breakfast. Promise you'll come right back?"

The uncertainty in Cam's expression hurt Dawn's heart. She moved to Cam and wrapped her arms around her neck. "I promise you I'll be back. We'll have breakfast and talk." She lightly touched her lips to Cam's. "I won't be gone long."

Cam was sliding the veggie omelets onto plates as Dawn returned. The dogs greeted her as though she'd been gone for days rather than the fifteen minutes or so that she'd been absent.

Dawn wrapped her arms around Cam and laid her head on her back. "Those omelets smell amazing. Plus fruit, toast, coffee, and orange juice…you're going to spoil me. How did you put all this together in the time it took me to get dressed?"

Cam shrugged. "It's just breakfast."

"If this is *just* breakfast, I can't wait to see when you make something special."

"Stick around and you just might find out." Cam's expression was unreadable.

"Do you think I won't?"

"I hope you do, but you seemed to be doing some pretty heavy thinking earlier and I'm worried that we jumped into something last night and you don't know what it means for you or us. Part of me feels like maybe I took advantage of you while you were vulnerable, and if I did, I'm sorry."

Only the sincerity and vulnerability in Cam's eyes kept Dawn's frustration at bay. "First, you did not take advantage of me. There is nothing for you to be sorry about. I made the first move last night, and even after I did, you gave me more than one opportunity to stop or slow down. If anything I think it was me that took advantage of you. I told you my story yesterday because I trust you. I know you're a good person and I feel safe with you. I was thinking a lot of things this morning. But if any part of it was regret, it was only because I waited so long for us to be together."

"Dawn, I—"

"Let me finish. I don't know where this is going and I'm not sure I need or even want to know that right now. What I do know is I've enjoyed getting to know you. You've been a really good friend. I care about you. And I *really* want to have more sex with you."

Cam sat silently for a moment, either processing what Dawn had said or waiting to make sure Dawn was finished this time, maybe both. Finally, she said, "Sounds good to me."

"Good. Glad we're on the same page."

That evening, after painting for most of the day, Dawn stood at her back window. From her vantage point, she could just see over the fence. Cam played with Mozz and Jack next door. She had a strong urge to join them. If she let herself, it would be so easy to imagine building a life with Cam. She wasn't ready to make that leap yet. They had just begun discovering one another. Dawn didn't want to rush things. Not that there was any danger of that given their history so far. When her doorbell rang, she reluctantly turned away from Cam.

Dawn's hand was poised on the doorknob when she peeked through the peephole out of habit. Both her hand and the blood in her veins froze. Lori. *How did she find me?* She couldn't move, she couldn't even think. Lori pounding on the door yanked her out of her haze and she reached for her phone, opened an app, and started recording. "Dawn, open up, I know you're in there?"

She couldn't possibly know that. Could she?

"Please open the door. All I want to do is talk." Lori's voice was less forceful and more controlled than it had been a moment earlier.

Dawn still didn't want to let her in to her home. She did not open the door. "Lori, go away. I don't want you here."

"Come on, babe, you don't mean that."

"You and I no longer have a relationship. We haven't for more than two years after the last time you beat me up."

"You know that was a misunderstanding."

"I know it wasn't. How did you find me anyway?"

Lori laughed mirthlessly. "You think it was hard to follow you home Friday night? Now open the door. We need to talk."

"That's not going to happen. If you don't leave right now, I'm calling the police."

"Don't do that. All I want to do is talk, but if you won't talk to me, I guess I'll have to go have a little chat with your lover next door. That's right. I know she's over there playing with her dogs. If you won't talk to me I'll go over there and deal with her directly."

Dawn opened the door a few inches, not even far enough for the chain to engage, making sure her foot was braced behind it. "Lori, she has nothing to do with you and me. Leave her alone."

"Either we can talk or she and I can. It's up to you."

"No."

"Okay, then I'll just say this…Either you stop seeing her or I'm going to go next door next time. You and I belong together. Right now she's in the way."

"I don't belong to anyone. Now leave. I'm calling the police." Dawn held up her phone and dialed 911. Before she pushed the button to connect the call, Lori turned and left. Dawn closed the door and sank to the floor.

She didn't know how long she'd been there when the doorbell rang again. Her heart leapt to her throat. She stood on shaky legs and peered through the peephole. Cam. After a few deep, cleansing breaths to ease her frayed nerves, she unchained the lock and opened the door. Before she could say anything, Cam spoke.

"Are you okay? I just saw Lori leave."

"I'm fine now, but it's sweet of you to check on me."

"I wasn't aiming for sweet. I was afraid for you. Did she hurt you?"

"No. I'm not hurt. I didn't let her in the house. Come in. You should probably hear what she had to say."

As Cam followed her to the couch, Dawn considered how much to tell her. She decided Cam deserved to hear all of it. After all, Lori had threatened her too. Sitting next to Cam on the sofa, Dawn drew strength from her. Although she figured she couldn't allow herself to do that for much longer. She wouldn't put Cam in danger. "I made a recording. I thought it might be useful later. I haven't listened to it yet. Can I now with you?"

"Of course."

Cam listened to the audio. She clenched her fists. Dawn tenderly rubbed Cam's knuckles still raw from the day before. "I told you I'm not looking for a white knight."

"I know. You're no damsel in distress, but everyone can use a hand every now and then. I want you to feel like you can call me if you need me."

"I do."

"Good. So, what's your plan? Do you think we should call the police?"

Dawn was grateful Cam wasn't jumping in with suggestions. She was letting her take the lead. She realized she was still stroking Cam's knuckles. She pulled her hand back and stood so she wouldn't be tempted to reach for her again. She paced in front of the couch. "If she comes back, I will call the police. Aside from that, I'm not entirely sure, but I think I'll start with filing a restraining order. You should look into it as well since she threatened you too."

"I'll think about it."

"Please don't do anything stupid. This isn't your fight."

"I won't go looking for her, but if she comes after you or me, I'll do what I have to do."

Dawn was too spent to argue the point. "Fair enough."

Cam stood and reached to push a stray strand of hair behind Dawn's ear. When Dawn flinched, she dropped her hand. "You sure you're okay?"

"I will be. I'm just fading pretty quickly now that the adrenaline has stopped pumping. I'm going to call it an early night."

"I could come back after I get the pups settled."

"No." Dawn met Cam's eyes. "I need some time to think."

"Take the time you need, but remember I'm right next door. I'm not going anywhere. Lori doesn't scare me for my sake, but I'm worried about you."

"I'll be fine. Thank you for checking on me. Good night."

"Good night, Dawn."

Cam stepped onto the porch and waited to hear the chain slip into place before she went down the steps. She drew in a lungful of air, hoping to ease the ache in her chest. Cam feared what Dawn wasn't saying. Dawn had already started to pull away from her, and she was at a loss as to how to stop that from happening. After their night together, Cam had been afraid something like this would happen. She was scared Dawn would change her mind. But when they talked at breakfast this morning, Dawn had eased her fears.

Now they were back with a vengeance. Cam didn't know if Dawn was pulling away because of what Lori might do, or if her own fears were clouding everything and Dawn really did just need some time to process everything. An asshole like Lori didn't deserve to be in the same room as Dawn. If there was anything she could do to stop Lori from hurting Dawn ever again, she would do whatever it took. Even if it meant walking away.

The mere thought of losing Dawn made her gut tighten, but she would willingly walk away rather than see Dawn hurt. She'd survive if what Dawn needed most was for Cam to let her go. She could give her time. They had been here before and moved beyond it. She wanted Dawn in her life but if that put Dawn at risk then she'd do whatever needed to be done to make sure she was safe.

CHAPTER SIXTEEN

Dawn found it remarkably easy to file a restraining order or an order of protection as they called it at the courthouse. Once she picked up a copy of her medical records from two years ago, and armed with her recording of Lori from the day before, she arrived at the courthouse expecting an arduous process. But there were advocates ready and willing to assist her every step of the way. By the time she left, she had a TRO, or temporary restraining order, in her hand and a hearing scheduled in ten days to see about making it more permanent.

Once she returned home, Dawn took stock of her life. She tried to seek solace in her gardens. When she was completely honest with herself, she could admit something essential was missing in her life. Her painting and gardening fulfilled her deeply creative spirit. Her sister and parents filled the strong familial bonds she'd always needed. Wonderful friends allowed her the freedom to be herself and to never have to apologize for being who she was. Her work at the shelter gave her a way to give back to those who had helped her. But when she was alone at night, something or, more precisely, someone was missing. There was no one to turn to, no one to share her most intimate thoughts and feelings. Nobody was there to touch her or for her to reach out and savor.

Dawn shook off the melancholy thoughts that plagued her all morning and tried to concentrate on her gardening. She was in love with Cam. She thought about that. If it wasn't true, she knew she wouldn't have slept with her. But now Cam was in danger because of Lori. She needed to pull back and gain some perspective, not only about how she wanted to move forward with Cam but she needed to figure out what to do about Lori. She didn't want Cam hurt because of her. That much she knew for sure.

She stood and brushed the dirt off her pants. If she couldn't enjoy gardening, she might as well give it up for now and try to be productive somewhere else. She gathered her bucket and headed to the back door. After discarding her gardening tools and hat, she quickly showered. Then, she pondered her next tasks. She wanted to see Cam. *No way,* the last rational part of her brain screamed. So much for distance, she thought. She needed a distraction, something to keep her from what was already distracting her, Cam. She reached for the phone and called her sister. Voice mail. *Damn.* So much for Ali's help. Dawn tried her parents next. Success.

"Hi, honey. This is a nice surprise."

"Hi, Mom, how are you?"

"We're fine and dandy. Your father says hello."

"Tell him hi back."

"Dawn, it's not that I don't like hearing from you out of the blue, but you don't usually call during the week. Are you okay?"

"I'm fine. I was just thinking about you and Daddy and thought I should check in."

"Any idea when you might get over this way for a proper visit? It seems like forever since we saw you."

Dawn thought about her schedule. Then, inspiration struck. "Why don't I come see you now?"

"What? You can't just fly across the country at a moment's notice."

"Why not? The art show's over. I have nothing pressing on my plate for a couple of weeks, and it's been too long since I saw you and Dad. Would it be okay if I come as soon as I can find a flight?"

"Well, of course it would, honey, but are you sure you're all right?"

"I'm fine, Mom. It would just be good to get away for a little while, and I can't think of any place I'd rather go."

"We're always happy to have you. When you find out the details, let me know and I'll have your father pick you up at the airport."

"Thanks. I'll call you back in a little while. I love you."

"I love you, too."

Dawn stared at her phone as she laid it on the table. *What the hell? Well, that certainly qualifies as a distraction.* While she got online to book a ticket she tried to convince herself she wasn't running away. She just needed time to think, and it would be much easier to do that from a distance. *Yeah, right, I'm so running away.*

❖

For about a second, Dawn considered simply sending Cam a text that she was headed to her parents. She realized that was unfair. Not only because of what they had recently shared but also if she disappeared, especially so soon after Lori's threats, Cam would worry. She could only hope Cam would understand.

A few minutes after Cam got home, Dawn texted, "Have a few minutes to chat? I could come over."

"Of course. I'm out back with the boys."

Dawn walked through the gate between their yards. Her carefully planned words flew out of her head when she saw Cam. She tried to focus on something else, so she could think. She bent down to pet the dogs who'd come to say hello. The tree Cam had finished planting the day before caught her attention. "Oh wow, that is perfect there."

"Yeah, it really turned out nicely."

Dawn turned back to Cam. "So, hi."

"Hi."

Dawn could feel the distance between them and blamed nobody but herself. As much as she wanted to close the distance, both metaphorical and physical, she didn't. She wasn't sure what she wanted and she didn't want to confuse the issue any more. She needed to say what she came for and get out of here.

"So…I've decided to go visit my parents for a few days."

Cam took a hesitant step toward Dawn and stopped. "Oh. Okay."

"I decided this morning when I was on the phone with my mom."

"Is everything okay with your parents?"

"Yes, they're fine. I just…need to get away for a little while." When Cam flinched Dawn realized her choice of words left a lot to be desired. She wasn't explaining things at all how she'd planned.

"When do you leave?"

"I'm catching the red-eye tonight."

"Wow. Okay. Do you need a ride to the airport?"

"That's sweet, but I thought I'd take a Lyft."

Cam's jaw clenched. "Great. Sounds like you've got it all figured out."

"Not at all."

"What?"

Dawn took a step forward cutting the distance between them in half. "I don't have anything figured out. My head's pretty messed up right now. Having Lori reappear in my life has thrown me for a loop. Add on everything that's happening between you and me, and as wonderful as it is, it's a lot to process. I need some time. I need to be away from all of it for a little while. Does that make any sense?"

"I understand. I really do, but that doesn't mean I have to like it."

"Thank you."

"For?"

"Being you. Understanding. Giving me the time and space I need."

"Promise me one thing."

"If I can."

"While you're out on that big farm, thinking serious thoughts, promise me you won't make any final decisions about you and me without coming home and having a conversation with me first."

"I give you my word."

Tuesday morning as the plane landed at Raleigh/Durham International Airport and taxied to the gate, Dawn stayed in her seat and let the other passengers deplane ahead of her. For once, she had packed light and hadn't checked any luggage. She'd left some extra clothes at the farm last time she visited, and if she needed anything else, she'd borrow it from her mom. As she waited, she studied the sunrise over the tarmac out the tiny airplane window.

In a couple of hours, she would be at her childhood home. She'd always found the hills of North Carolina peaceful. She only hoped she could still find the peace within herself since her mind was so jumbled with everything happening with Cam and Lori. She wanted to spend some time on the farm with her parents. Maybe she would go hiking. All she had was time.

She dashed off a quick text and then she called Cam. She couldn't decide what it meant that she missed her already.

"Hello?"

"Good morning, I hope I didn't wake you?"

"You didn't. I'm getting ready for work. Are you there?"

"Yeah, still at the airport. Wanted to let you know I'd landed safely."

"I appreciate that. I hope you enjoy time with your parents and that you get what you need from your trip."

"Thank you. I just sent you a text. That's my parents' number. I forgot to tell you cell coverage is spotty at their place. So, if you need me for anything, use that number."

"Okay. Just so you know, I probably won't use it."

"Why not?"

"Two reasons. A big project is launching at work today and I'm going to be working crazy hours this week. But most importantly, you asked for space and I will respect that."

"Okay. Well…like I said, you have it if you need it. I should go."

"Good-bye, Dawn."

"Bye."

On some level, Dawn was certain Cam's last words were simply a salutation. What everyone said at the end of a phone call. But her inflection sounded so…final. Maybe Cam was tired of waiting for her to make up her mind after all. Cam had been so patient for so long, maybe it had finally become too much. Certainly she would have said something when they'd talked the day before. There was nothing she could do from here other than call her back. But until she knew for sure what she wanted, she doubted that was a good idea.

She was here for time and space. Cam would have the same while she was away. She'd only just realized that. She wasn't entirely sure how she felt about it. She didn't know what Cam was thinking about all this. She hadn't asked. When had she become so selfish? So many questions to answer and she wasn't going to figure out anything while sitting on the tarmac.

By the time she turned away from the window, the plane was nearly empty. She grabbed her carry-on and headed into the terminal. Her dad would be waiting. She strode purposefully to their appointed meeting spot outside the departure doors. In her dad's estimation it was easier to find someone waiting on the curb when every other person was headed inside. Mere moments after Dawn arrived, she saw him. She raised her hand in a casual wave as he pulled up to the curb in his old Ford pickup.

Dawn hopped into the truck, threw her bag behind the seat, and scooted over to wrap her arms around her father. It might have been an impromptu visit, but the moment she saw him, she realized how much she truly missed her parents. "Hi, Dad."

He wrapped his right arm tightly around her. He cleared his throat before he said, "Hi, your mother wants me to ask you first thing if you're really all right?"

Dawn pulled back far enough so she could look into his eyes. His face was perpetually red from the sun, and he had deep crow's feet around his eyes from all his time outdoors without sunglasses. But his brown eyes were clear and sparkled with the intelligence he had never felt the need to flaunt. Dawn shrugged. She'd never been able to keep anything from him. The one or two times she had tried, he'd known there was more. He patiently waited until she told him. "I'm fine, Dad. At least physically there isn't anything wrong. I just have a lot on my mind and needed some time away from everything to try to get some perspective."

He gave a slight nod. "Okay. Buckle up, Buttercup."

Dawn grinned at the nickname her dad had always used for her as she followed his instruction and clicked her seat belt closed. He wouldn't press and she loved him for it. But he was also a great listener and might be able to give her an unbiased read on the whole Cam situation. "I'd like to tell you a story."

"Okay," he said as he made his way to the airport exit and headed for the interstate.

By the time her dad drove down the dirt road to the farm nearly two hours later, Dawn had told him everything about Cam and also what had happened with Lori. She didn't spare any details. He knew her almost as well as Ali did, and even though he didn't know all the details about her past relationships, he knew enough to understand her hesitation at becoming involved with another woman. Her father turned to her. "So, to sum it up… You ran away from your current home back to your first home to escape the reach of a crazy ex. But you also ran away from another woman who has done nothing but be open, thoughtful, and respectful."

"Yeah, pretty much. Cam is all of those things and more. I can't get her out of my head, but I'm not sure I can truly let her into my life, either."

"Can I ask you something?"

"Of course."

"If someone driving a car is stopped at a red light and gets rear-ended, is the person in the car who gets hit at fault?"

Dawn had no idea where her father was going with this. "Of course not."

"And if a month later, the same driver who got hit is driving along, following all the rules of the road goes through a green light and gets T-boned, is it that driver's fault?"

"No, it's not. I don't understand your point."

"I'm getting there, bear with me. So, the same driver has been in two accidents in one month, but neither occurrence was her fault. Should she stop driving?"

"She might want to, given her luck, but no, she did nothing wrong."

"Neither did you, Dawn."

"What are you talking about?"

"You were hurt, more than once. Are you going to continue to let the women who hurt you stop you from getting where you want to go? Are you going to hide from the world, or Cam specifically, and never risk the possibility of getting hurt again even if you might find something worth the risk if you went for it?"

What could she possibly say? He was right.

"You've given me something to think about but I'm still not sure what I'm going to do."

"Well, right this minute I reckon you should go say hi to your mama. We'll talk more later on. Don't worry about your bag. I'll get it."

"Thanks, Dad."

As Dawn jumped from the truck, her mom walked onto the front porch, the screen door slamming behind her. Her red hair, so much like Dawn's, was just beginning to gray at the temples. Her eyes sparkled with welcome and love. The apron she wore brought back so many fond memories of Dawn's childhood. Dawn vaulted up the stairs and grabbed her in a fierce hug. "Hi, Mom."

"Hi, honey. I'm just finishing a pie. Why don't you join me and you can fill me in on what's going on and why you're really here."

From behind Dawn, her dad deadpanned, "That could take a while."

Dawn wrapped an arm around her mom's waist and chuckled. "It really could. I talked dad's ear off the whole way home."

"I don't care how long it takes, I want to hear everything. Once I get this pie in the oven, I'll make you breakfast."

"Lead the way," Dawn said and prepared to repeat the saga that was her life the last few months.

By the time Dawn got through her story a second time, breakfast was done and she and her mom sat in rocking chairs on the back porch with a clear view of the pasture and garden. She stifled another yawn. "Honey, it sounds like Cam's a very nice woman. We'll talk more about her later, but you must be exhausted. Why don't you go on up to your room and take a nap?"

"That's okay. I want to walk around the barns and stuff." As she covered her third yawn in as many minutes, Dawn changed course. "Maybe a nap would be a good idea. I haven't been sleeping all that well."

"Not surprising with everything going on. Now, go on up and get settled in. If you're not down by lunchtime, I'll wake you."

"Thanks, Mom, I love you."

"I love you, too. I'm glad you're here."

Dawn leaned down and kissed her mom on the cheek. "Me too."

When she reached her childhood bedroom, she found her bag where her dad had laid it on her bed. She set it aside, kicked off her shoes, shimmied out of her jeans, and crawled beneath the handmade quilt on the twin bed. She closed her eyes and all she could see was Cam. Maybe it was the distance or talking about her for hours with her parents, but for some reason seeing Cam as she closed her eyes to sleep didn't scare her today. In fact she found comfort in it. She allowed her mind to focus on Cam and drifted off to sleep. When she woke she realized she'd slept better than she had in weeks.

❖

Tuesday morning Cam stood in her backyard playing with her dogs. She was surprised when Dawn had called to let her know she'd arrived safely. Cam hadn't really expected to hear from her at all. She wondered if that said more about her feelings or Dawn's. As she surveyed the yard, she became more and more irritated. Every plant, flower, and tree in her yard made her think of Dawn. She was three thousand miles away and still she invaded her thoughts.

When Dawn told her she was leaving town, Cam said she understood and part of her did. But the other parts of her were angry and frustrated that Dawn didn't stay and fight, that she hadn't leaned on Cam for support. Dawn wasn't alone this time. Cam would have stood beside her to face Lori. Clearly, either Dawn didn't trust that or it wasn't enough.

Eventually, Cam realized Dawn might have left town to protect her. Cam hoped that wasn't the case, but she knew it was. This was Dawn protecting her and taking the time she needed. Two birds, one stone. Cam didn't need protection from a bully like Lori. It hurt Cam much more to think Dawn wouldn't turn to her for help with something like this. Their friendship had been growing steadily stronger for months but at the first sign of trouble, Dawn abandoned her.

When the dogs tired of chasing the ball she'd been throwing, Cam flopped onto the grass. Mozz laid his head on her leg. She petted him and thought out loud. "I've given her nothing but time. I'm not sure how much longer I can keep doing it. I wish she'd talked to me about her fears and not run away. What type of relationship can we build if she can't trust me?"

Cam wasn't sure if she could go back to just being friends with Dawn. Maybe it was better to back off and let things take their natural course. "Maybe I just need to move on. I'm not even sure what our relationship is anyway? She cares for me and wants more sex. That's what she said. So what...we're friends with benefits? I don't think that's enough for me. But I still want Dawn in my life." Mozz simply scratched his ear and panted. He was no help at all.

There was nothing she could do about it right now anyway. Hopefully, the research and work for her work project would keep her busy enough to stop the circular thoughts about Dawn. If she could focus on work she didn't have to think about anything or anyone else. Fat chance of that, but what choice did she have? The next move was Dawn's.

❖

Dawn spent several days wandering around the farm. She visited the animals in the barn and passed time with the goats, horses, and pigs. She especially loved meeting all the babies that had been born this spring. Her favorite was the newest kid. He was already so rambunctious. He came right up to her and butted her leg. But when she scratched his head he calmed down.

She drove the tractor, fed the chickens, gathered eggs, helped her dad mend a fence, and baked bread with her mom. She spent lazy afternoons napping in the hayloft. She sketched things around the farm—tractors, the barn, trees, and many of the animals, but she also drew the face she saw in vivid color on the film screen of her eyelids whenever she closed her eyes. Her sketchbook was more than half full of Cam. Then, she spent two more days hiking a part of the Appalachian Trail near her parents' farm.

The one thing that became clear during her time away was that she couldn't stop thinking about Cam. That didn't make her feel more certain about anything. Cam wasn't Lori. Dawn had to believe that she couldn't have fallen in love with Cam if she was anything like Lori. She wanted to trust herself and her judgment of Cam's character, but how could she be sure? She'd fallen for Lori too. Lori had been kind and patient at the beginning. How could she truly know if things wouldn't change between her and Cam if they moved forward with a relationship?

She had only seen Cam frustrated one time and she hadn't turned that on Dawn, she'd simply left the room. The only time she'd seen Cam really angry, she'd taken it out on the heavy bag and her own knuckles. But that had, in some way, been to fight for Dawn, to beat up her enemies, even if it had only been in Cam's head.

She thought about when they'd gone bowling and Cam had been playful even as she lost. That was something Lori would never have been able to do. It also occurred to her that after fifteen months of dating, she'd never given Lori her parents' number.

But she had given it to Cam when she landed in Raleigh. Clearly, she trusted Cam more than she realized.

Dawn had to face reality. She couldn't hide in North Carolina forever. Cam was sweet, patient, and kind. Dawn wasn't sure she deserved Cam. She had promised to talk to her before she made a final decision and she could give her that at least.

Chapter Seventeen

When Dawn landed in San Diego the first thing she needed to do was see Cam. She'd made Cam a promise before she left and she needed to talk to her. She went over to Cam's and rang the bell. When she got no answer, she settled on sending a text to Cam. "Hi, I'm home. Do you have any time to talk this evening?"

"Hi. I'm probably working late, but I can let you know when I get home and you're welcome to come over."

"Sounds like a plan. Have a good day."

"You too."

She only stopped in the house long enough to throw her bag on the bed and change into clothes she didn't care about getting dirty. She and her gardens needed some weeding time.

Since she'd been gone nearly a week, her yard was in desperate need of attention. She attacked the gardens in the backyard first. She noticed that she didn't hear Mozz or Jack playing out back, then refocused on weeding. When the sun was directly above her, Dawn sat back on her heels and surveyed her yard. She had the back under control. She grabbed a glass of cold lemonade and headed for the front yard. By the time she was finished, after six in the evening, Cam still hadn't come home.

By the time the text from Cam finally came it was almost eight o'clock. Dawn was on pins and needles waiting to see her.

"Finally home. Still want to come over?"

"Yes, if that's okay?"

"Sure."

Cam opened the door and stepped back so Dawn could enter. Cam appeared drawn and worn out like she hadn't slept in days. The dark circles under her eyes gave her a haunted look. A strong urge to comfort Cam gripped her. She took a step toward Cam but stopped short when Cam's body stiffened. "Cam, are you okay?"

"I'm fine, just tired. How was your trip?"

"It was nice."

"Good."

As the silence stretched between them, Dawn wasn't sure what to do. She'd had a plan, but Cam's reaction threw her off. Courage was a funny thing. When you don't need it, you think you'll have enough to draw on when you do. When it came time and you needed courage, often there was no time to think about whether you had enough. You just jumped in or ran away. Cam seemed to be the jump in type. Dawn wasn't sure she had the courage to stand and face what she needed to. She wanted to be with Cam. Sometimes, that thought alone had her looking for the closest escape route. It terrified her to care that much about one person.

How could she possibly tell Cam the truth and give her so much power? She'd never be able to protect herself from the pain. If she hid the truth, she was a coward, but she'd shield herself from the gut-wrenching blow that seemed to be inevitable in all her significant romantic relationships. The idea left her hollow. Was it possible that not telling Cam she wanted her could hurt Dawn even more than the pain she expected down the road?

She thought about the last few months. From the instant attraction she and Cam had for each other to the first tentative steps Cam took toward something more, to her surrender at Dawn's resistance, and her insistence that being friends was all she wanted. Cam had loved and lost in a devastating way, yet she was willing to put herself back out there, open to the possibility of finding love again. Cam never hid how she felt about Dawn, but she'd backed off and allowed Dawn the safety and comfort of friendship without the pressure of something more.

Dawn knew she had changed. She had started to open up and even believe something more might be possible for her one day. The big question was…did she have the courage to be honest with Cam and see where the truth would lead them.

Dawn's heart raced. Perhaps she was too late, but she had to try. She stared into Cam's questioning eyes and gave her the only thing she could, the truth. "I missed you."

Cam exhaled as she sank into the cushions. She laid her head on the back and closed her eyes like she was either in pain or savoring something, and Dawn was worried because she couldn't tell which. This time when Dawn moved to Cam, she didn't stop until she was settled beside her on the couch. She sat as close as she could without touching her. "Cam?"

"Did you get what you needed out of the trip?"

"I'm still worried about what Lori might do. But I did have the time I needed to think…about you, about us."

"And?"

"And I realized I want you in my life as more than a friend, even more than a friend with benefits. Cam, I'd like…I'd like to see you. For us to really see if what I'm feeling is real and sustainable."

Cam let out a long, slow breath.

Dawn wasn't aware that she'd reached out and put her hand on Cam's leg until she felt Cam stiffen. She moved to pull away, but Cam caught her hand and kept it on her leg with her own hand firmly covering it. The connection felt good. It felt right. She wished she could read Cam's expression.

They sat in silence for a few minutes. Dawn was a little worried that Cam hadn't said anything, but she was willing to give her time. She finally said, "Did you finish the project?"

Cam absently swept her thumb over Dawn's hand. "Yeah, about three this morning."

"Then you worked all day?"

Cam nodded. "I had to get caught up on everything that had been pushed aside while the project was the priority."

"You must be exhausted."

"Exhausted doesn't even begin to cover it." Cam shook her head slightly, but she never took her eyes off Dawn.

"I should let you get some sleep."

"You don't need to leave."

Dawn turned her hand which rested under Cam's, and their fingers intertwined automatically. "I do. I need to be up early for the hearing about the permanent restraining order."

"Oh, is that tomorrow? Would you like me to go with you?"

"It's sweet of you to ask, but I feel like this is something I need to do on my own."

"I guess I can understand that."

"If you don't have plans Friday night, why don't I see if Kate and June are free and we can go out to dinner?"

Cam's smile finally reached her tired eyes. "That would be great."

"Good. Now get some sleep." Dawn kissed Cam lightly on the mouth and then stood. "Sweet dreams, Cam."

Dawn couldn't sleep. She wandered aimlessly around her studio looking at different pieces she had painted, old and new. A number of her paintings had sold at the show, quite a few. The ones she'd painted recently were around the studio waiting for her to decide what to do with them. She was struck by how much more color there was in her recent works; they were brighter.

She wondered for a moment what had changed. A picture of Cam formed in her mind. Dawn admitted to herself she was in love with Cam, and no matter what happened between them that would be true until the day she died. She owed it to Cam to tell her the truth. She owed it to both of them. But she didn't want to tell her until there was nothing standing between them.

Cam had reawakened parts of her that she thought were gone. Pieces she thought she had buried years before. Cam resuscitated feelings Dawn wasn't so sure she had wanted brought out into the open again. But she couldn't deny the evidence in front of her. Cam inspired her to find the light in herself. Dawn placed a blank canvas on her main easel, mixed her paints, and let the inspiration flow until the sun crept low on the horizon.

Dawn did not relish going to court for the hearing to make the restraining order permanent, but it needed to be done. She spent extra time on her makeup and dressed in one of her best suits leftover from her banking days as though arming herself for battle. According to the advocate she'd spoken with when she filed the TRO, Lori had a right to be there so she braced herself for that possibility.

Dawn expected old feelings to overwhelm her when she saw Lori. When they didn't, she let out a long, silent sigh. "Hi, Lori," she said. She studied Lori. Objectively, she could see Lori was still physically attractive, but Dawn felt no connection to her anymore.

"Come on, baby, it's time to call this off so we can get back together. Surely you're not still mad at me for what happened years ago."

It shouldn't have surprised her at all that Lori viewed what happened between them as something Dawn would simply get over. She shook her head, not because she was sad about what she planned to say to Lori but because of how much time she let what happened with Lori affect her life. "No, Lori. It's over and has been for a long time. I have no desire to get back together with you. No matter how many times you show up where I am that isn't going to change. I don't care what you do or say any more. I don't care why you did what you did and I don't want to hear your excuses. I came here to make sure you stay away from me."

Dawn could tell Lori didn't believe her. "Dawn, I will always be your first. You will never forget me. Even if you're sleeping with someone else, like your bitch neighbor, I will always be in your head. You will eventually come back to me because I love you more than anyone else ever will."

Dawn realized how pathetic it all was and felt just a little sorry for Lori. "No, Lori, you don't. What you call love was control and you no longer have any control over me. You will always be my first female lover. There is nothing I can do to change that. But you will never be my last or my best lover. There is only one thing I will think about you, if I think about you at all, and that is you opened my eyes to a whole new world. I will always be grateful for that. But I no longer care about anything else that happened between us, and it's sad to me that after two years you haven't moved on."

Lori crossed her arms defensively. "I've moved on."

"You haven't or you wouldn't have showed up at my opening, come to my house, or tried to come between me and Cam. You wouldn't have threatened her. Now I'm going to talk to the judge so you can't ever be close to us again. If you ever come near either one of us, ever, we'll have you arrested. Now move on for real and leave us alone."

Dawn walked away and didn't look back. As she spoke to the judge, she was aware that Lori fumed a few rows back. Once the judge granted the permanent restraining order, Dawn left the courtroom. She did not even glance in Lori's direction. *Free at last.*

❖

Dawn had just finished changing out of her suit when the doorbell rang. Slightly worried that it would be Lori, she made sure to check the peephole. Cam. She pulled the door open. "Come in. Not working today?"

"Working from home, but I saw you pull in. I wanted to see how the hearing went."

"Pretty much as expected, the judge issued a permanent restraining order."

"Oh good."

"Lori was there."

"Oh?"

"Yeah, she approached me before the hearing and tried to convince me to call it all off and to get back together with her."

"How was that for you?"

"It was much easier than I thought it would be. I think a part of me used to be scared that she would be able to convince me to go back to her if I ever spoke to her. But I wasn't afraid of that anymore. I am grateful I had some of those experiences. Obviously not the abuse, although it did make me realized how strong I am. But the relationship, in general, helped me figure out who I was and who I am. Once I said what I needed to say to her, I walked away. When I left the courthouse, it felt exactly like the closure I was looking for."

"Why weren't you afraid you would give in to her anymore?"

"I went there this morning knowing she no longer has any power over me." Dawn finally moved to Cam. "I knew it because I'm in love with someone else."

Cam opened her mouth and then shut it without saying anything.

Dawn took Cam's hand in hers and gazed into her eyes. "Cam, I've known for a while that I'm in love with you. But I owed it to you and to myself to be absolutely sure before I said anything. One of the things I figured out while I was out of town is I had to face the fact that no matter where I went, no matter how far away I tried to get, I couldn't get you out of my mind. I couldn't hide forever. I needed to come home, back to my life, back to my work, and most importantly, back to you. Seeing Lori confirmed what I already knew. I never loved her the way I love you. My feelings for her were like a schoolgirl crush compared to the way I feel about you. It felt like more at the time because it was so new and foreign. Lori hurt me badly, but now I realize I can't let that stop me from living my life. I deserve to live a life full of love and laughter. I forgot that for a long time.

"But with you, I couldn't stop it, you know I tried. I didn't want anything to happen between us because I was scared I would be hurt again. I didn't want to feel anything for you. I knew from the day I met you that you had the power to hurt me if I let you. But you were so patient and you became my friend and you just let me get to know you and showed me time and again that you would never hurt me intentionally. Now I love everything about you. I only hope I didn't wait too long to figure it out."

"How long?" She cleared her throat and tried again. "How long have you known?"

"Since the day I told you about Lori."

Cam's face betrayed her surprise. "Why didn't you tell me?"

"I wanted to, more than you can imagine. After the way I acted for so long, stubbornly refusing to even entertain the idea of a relationship or even agree to a date, I didn't think there was any way you would believe me. I had to earn your trust just like you earned mine. So I offered you what I could that day. I gave you my story. Then as you know, one thing led to another. Having mind-blowing sex with you, and then Lori showing up threatening to hurt you…it was a lot to process. I hadn't even figured out where I wanted to go with you, other than probably have more sex, because again, wow. I needed time."

"And now, what are you offering me now?"

Dawn closed the remaining distance between them, not scared anymore of jumping off the ledge. "My heart, my body, everything I am. My heart belongs to you. Please tell me it's not too late."

She lowered her head to Dawn's. "Oh, Dawn, it's definitely not too late." She pulled Dawn into her arms and crushed her mouth to Dawn's.

Dawn returned fire with fire. She could not wait to get Cam's hands on her again.

Cam ended the kiss and lifted her head. "In case you haven't figured it out already, I'm in love with you too. I have been for a long time."

"I hoped."

"I have a question for you."

"You can ask me anything."

"Will you please let me cook dinner for you now?"

Dawn laughed out loud. Of all the things Cam might have asked, she hadn't expected that. "That sounds like a date."

"It was meant to."

"In that case, I would like that very much."

"Great. I have a few things I need to finish first, so how about you come over around seven?" Cam said.

"Wonderful. I'll see you then."

"Just one thing before I go." Cam's lips were gentler this time, savoring. The heat was no less intense. "That might hold me. See you at seven."

Chapter Eighteen

By the time Dawn rang the doorbell at seven sharp, dinner preparation was well under way. Cam opened the door and pulled Dawn inside.

"I missed you," Cam said.

"Me too. Will you kiss me now?"

Cam did, leaving them both breathless, chests heaving. Then she stepped back and linked her fingers with Dawn's to walk with her back to the kitchen. "How was your afternoon?"

"Wonderful. I started a new painting. How about yours?"

"Productive. Are you hungry?"

"Yes. It smells great."

"It's almost ready. I just need to boil the pasta for a couple of minutes. Wine?"

"Yes, please."

Cam handed Dawn a glass of chilled white wine.

"Thank you. Did you say anything to June or Kate about us?"

"Not yet. I pretty much focused on work the rest of the day, when I could keep my mind off you, that is."

Dawn sipped her wine. Cam continued to make her feel special. "You think it will surprise them?"

"I don't think so. I imagine there's a bet going on about when it would happen."

"You're kidding, right? Am I that obvious?"

"I think June and Kate could both see it headed in this direction."

"I'm sorry I made you wait so long."

"No need to apologize. You needed to get here in your own time."

Dawn stepped to Cam and wrapped her arms around her waist and laid her head on Cam's shoulder. "Thank you. I'm curious, how long would you have waited?"

"As long as it took. I'm not going to pretend it was easy. There were certainly times I wondered if you'd ever give me a chance. There were days I wasn't sure I could stand the waiting. But I didn't ever get to the point where I thought about looking for someone else, because every time I doubted anything would ever happen, I kept remembering you were worth the wait."

"I love you, Cam."

"I love you, too."

The shrimp scampi Cam prepared was delicious. Once Dawn had food in her and started a second glass of wine, she stifled a yawn, her sleepless night finally catching up with her.

"Tired?"

"Hmm, a little. Actually more than that. It's been a pretty eventful day and I didn't sleep much last night."

Cam stood and held out her hand. "Let me take you home. I'd ask you to stay, just to sleep, but we probably both need some time to process all that's happened today."

"You're right. I'm sorry. I should have taken a nap."

"You have nothing to be sorry about."

"I hoped the night would last longer."

Cam understood what she didn't say. As she walked Dawn across the yards Cam said, "There's no rush. We'll get back there eventually." Before Dawn could respond, Cam leaned down and kissed her, lingering over it. "Sweet dreams, my love."

Dawn smiled at the endearment. "Good night, Cam."

When Cam got back to her place, she pondered the last thirty-six hours. A lot had changed. Everything had changed. She was glad the evening had ended when it did. She needed time to adjust. Even though Dawn said she'd known for a while how she felt about Cam, she'd only let Cam in on it today. What if Dawn changed her mind again? It wasn't a possibility Cam wanted to think too hard about but she had to. She was certain her feelings for Dawn wouldn't change. She was less certain of Dawn's feelings for her. The best thing to do was take things slow and do what felt right.

❖

Cam stood on Dawn's porch and took a deep breath. They were about to go out on their first official date—granted it was a double date, but it was a beginning and she was nervous. She rang the bell.

Dawn answered the door in a pale green summer dress that left much of her pale skin exposed and complemented her eyes. "Hi."

Cam's mouth went dry. She cleared her throat. "Hi, you look beautiful."

"Thank you. Are those for me?"

Cam offered the gardening gloves in her hand. "It seems silly now, but I couldn't find any flowers to compare to yours and I thought you might find these useful."

"They're perfect." Dawn leaned over and kissed Cam lightly on the lips.

Cam relaxed into the soft kiss. She didn't need to be nervous with Dawn. As they broke apart, Cam said, "Your chariot awaits."

"Lead the way."

Cam held out her hand, Dawn clasped it, and they walked next door together.

Dawn slid into the truck next to Cam. "I'm glad we're doing this."

"Me too. Kate and June are meeting us at the restaurant?"

"Yes."

Cam took Dawn's hand and placed it on her thigh. "Did you tell them anything about what we discussed last night?"

"No, I thought maybe that was something you'd want to do together."

"Okay."

Once they were seated and had ordered drinks, they exchanged small talk for a few minutes. After their drinks arrived, Dawn cleared her throat. She reached for Cam's hand under the table. "So, Cam and I want you to know we're dating."

After a couple of seconds, Kate and June both started talking at once.

"About time. Congratulations."

"Finally."

"Tell us how you really feel," Dawn said.

"We're very happy for you," Kate said.

❖

When dinner was over, they walked out onto the sidewalk. The air had just begun to cool on the beautiful summer evening. Cam wasn't ready for the evening to end. "How about we leave the cars parked and walk down to Hillcrest Brewing Company?"

After exchanging a quick look, June said, "We're in."

"Dawn?"

"Sounds good to me."

Cam took Dawn's hand. "Great, let's go."

They had only gone the length of a few storefronts when Cam pulled up short. She glanced back. "Kate, get out your phone and be ready to call the police."

Kate said, "Okay. Why?"

Confusion washed across Dawn's face. "What's wrong?"

"We're about to have some company, and I don't want to take any chances." Cam nodded in the direction of the figure approaching them and closing the gap quickly.

The color drained from Dawn's face when she recognized Lori. "What are you doing here?"

"Really? You knew it would come to this. Wasn't very smart of you, Dawn," Lori said.

Without looking back, Dawn said, "Kate, would you make that call now? Let them know we need help enforcing a restraining order."

"Of course."

"Come on, baby, you don't have to do that," Lori pleaded.

"If you leave right now, we'll call them off."

"I'm not leaving without you."

Cam had stood silent long enough. She knew Dawn was strong enough to stand up to Lori. But Lori needed to know Cam would stand up for her too. She took a step toward her, angling her body so Dawn was behind her. Out of the corner of her eye, she saw June shift as well. "Yes, you are."

"Back up, bitch, this doesn't concern you."

"I think it does and you made sure of that. You threatened to come after me if Dawn didn't stop seeing me, but this doesn't concern me? Actually, it concerns me quite a lot. The police are on their way and you don't have much time if you want to get out of here."

"I'm not going anywhere. I haven't done anything wrong."

"You're in violation of the restraining order. But since we seem to have a few minutes, let me tell you how pathetic I think you are. How can you possibly hit someone you claim to love? It makes me sick even calling you a butch. You're a disgrace. You're pitiful."

Cam saw it coming, but she didn't duck. She allowed Lori's fist to land on her jaw but she absorbed most of the blow. Still, it was enough to split her lip and it stung quite bit. Cam stood there, blood trailing from the side of her mouth and down her chin. "Did that make you feel better?" She asked as she wiped her mouth with the back of her sleeve.

Cam sensed rather than saw June holding Dawn's arm, allowing her to handle the situation. Lori seethed, and as Cam put her arm back down to her side, Lori struck her again. She let another blow land, knowing she'd have a black eye by morning. But she also knew the officer in the patrol car had pulled up and witnessed at least the second punch. When Lori went to strike her again, she leaned right, grabbed her arm and pinned it behind her back. As Lori yelled obscenities at her, she addressed the cop. "Officer, I'd like to press charges for assault. This woman attacked me and is in violation of a restraining order."

Cam released Lori with the police officer there and stepped back.

"I saw those punches. You'll want to get some ice on your face soon, but I'll need to get your statements before you leave. Please don't go anywhere."

"Wouldn't think of it." The officer handcuffed Lori. She read her her rights as she walked her to the patrol car. Then Cam turned to Dawn who was shaking.

"What the hell were you thinking? I was handling it." Dawn stood toe to toe with Cam.

"You were, but she wasn't listening to you, and I wanted her to know I'm not afraid of her. She doesn't intimidate me. I also needed you to know I would stand up for you. I'll protect you."

"You said you wouldn't try to be a white knight. You egged her on. She could have really hurt you."

"I said I wouldn't track her down and I didn't. If I'd seen a weapon or even thought she had one, I would have handled the situation differently, but I knew I could beat her in a fair fight."

"Lori's lucky Cam didn't throw a punch," June said.

Dawn shot her a withering look and June took a step back and remained quiet.

"Why didn't you throw a punch?" Dawn asked.

"That would have defeated the whole purpose. If I'd knocked her down, she wouldn't be in a police car right now arrested for assault and I might be. I'm sorry if I scared you."

Dawn expelled a forceful breath. "I was only scared that she would hurt you."

"I hope this means she won't bother us again, but there's no way to know for sure."

"We'll be careful. Now let me look at your face." Dawn put her hands on Cam's cheeks and assessed the damage. "Oh, Cam, that looks like it hurts."

"It does, but it was well worth it if it gets her out of our lives."

Chapter Nineteen

"You're quiet," Cam said.

Dawn had barely noticed the scenery passing as she'd been preoccupied for the entire ride. Luckily Cam was driving. They'd been dating a little more than a week and were headed to Cindy and Lynn's for dinner. "I guess I'm a little nervous."

Cam took Dawn's hand and held it on her thigh. "Why? I thought you had a great time with Cindy and Lynn last time."

"I did. I like them both. It's just that…we weren't dating then."

"Why do you think that will change things? Cindy and Lynn both knew how I felt about you that time too."

Dawn shrugged. "I don't know. The two of them mean so much to you. What if I don't measure up?"

Cam squeezed Dawn's hand. "You don't have anyone to measure up to. I love you and you make me happy. That's all either of them care about. It'll be fine."

Dawn didn't answer. Cam was almost at the house and there wasn't any time to do anything about it anyway.

After climbing out of the truck, Cam took Dawn's hand again. But she stopped before going any farther. "Sweetheart, try to relax. It will be okay, I promise."

Cam had earned her trust and Dawn knew her word was good. "Okay, I'll try."

With Dawn's hand in hers, Cam walked to the house. She pushed open the front door and called out, "Hello."

Cindy called from the kitchen, "Come on back, you two." She dried her hands on a dish towel as Cam and Dawn came into the kitchen. She wrapped her arms around Dawn in a warm welcome. "So good to see you again."

The tension drained from Dawn's shoulders as she returned the hug. "You too."

"Would you like wine, beer?"

"I would love a glass of wine," Dawn said.

"I could go for a beer."

As Cindy reached for a wine glass and the bottle she had open on the counter, she said to Cam, "You know where the beer is. Help yourself. Would you take one out to Lynn and let her know you're here?"

Before answering, Cam turned to Dawn with a question in her eyes. When she saw Dawn's almost imperceptible nod, she said, "Sure, be right back." She grabbed two bottles from the refrigerator and headed out back.

Cindy handed a wineglass to Dawn and picked up her own. "Here's to new friends and new beginnings."

"I'll definitely drink to that." After sipping the wine, Dawn said, "That's lovely. It also smells amazing in here. What are you making?"

"I have lasagna Bolognese in the oven."

"Sounds delicious. Cam said you love to cook."

"It's one of my favorite things. What about you?"

"I can barely boil water most days. Someday, I would like to learn how to make a few dishes. It would be nice to be able to make dinner for Cam sometimes."

"I could teach you, if you want."

"Really? That would be awesome." Dawn made sure Cam was still out back. "Do you think we could keep it just between us for now? I would love to surprise Cam."

Cindy smiled. "I think that's a fantastic idea. Let's set something up before you leave tonight."

Dawn only nodded as both of them heard Cam and Lynn coming in the back door.

"It's great to see you again, Dawn," Lynn said.

"You too." Dawn met Cam's eyes across the room.

They had a nice, comfortable dinner. After dinner, while Cam and Lynn did the dishes, Cindy showed Dawn around the yard. Dawn was amazed by the land that housed chickens and goats. "I didn't realize you two had all this space back here. It reminds me a little of my parents' farm in North Carolina.

"We didn't start out to be farmers, but once we got the goats, we quickly realized we loved it. So it seemed natural to plant the huge garden and try to grow as much of our own food as possible. Of course, there was a pretty steep learning curve and the goats ended up eating most of our first harvest. Then, we figured out how to keep them penned in their own area. It's a lot of work, as I'm sure you know, but we both love being outdoors. Building something that is our own is special and makes every minute we spend out here worth the effort."

"I understand completely. Not only from growing up on a farm, but from spending time in my own gardens. I love it so much."

"I noticed your yard when I visited Cam. Your flowers are beautiful and the layout of your beds is intriguing."

"Thank you. Next time you come over, I'll show you the gardens in my backyard. In addition to having more perennials back there, I also grow vegetables."

"Sounds great."

❖

Cam glanced over at Dawn as she backed down the driveway. "How was that for you?"

"It was wonderful. I have no idea why I was so worried. Cindy and Lynn are fantastic and dinner was amazing."

"I'm glad you had a nice time. It's a beautiful night. How would you like to go for a walk on the beach?"

"I'd love to."

Cam and Dawn walked, talked, and kissed under the stars. It was indeed a beautiful night. The ride home was quiet. Cam walked Dawn across her yard and up onto her porch. Dawn opened her front door and turned to Cam. She wrapped her arms around her waist. "Will you come in?"

Cam put her forehead on Dawn's. "I'm sorry I can't tonight. I have to be up super early in the morning. Can I call you after work tomorrow?"

Dawn searched Cam's eyes wanting so much to know what was going on behind them. "Darling, you don't need to ask."

Cam kissed her sweetly. "I love you."

"I love you, Cam, sleep well."

"You too."

Cam crossed back to her yard before Dawn walked into the house and shut the door. She needed to ask Cam what was going on, but she was afraid to press her about something like this so soon into their relationship. They hadn't had sex since that first time, well, make that several times. Thinking back on it was still exciting. They were great together. So why did Cam seemingly not want to go there again? Maybe it hadn't been as good for her. Dawn knew Cam was turned on by her, but since then, she seemed to be avoiding getting in any situation that might lead to the bedroom. Dawn was starting cooking class with Cindy tomorrow. Maybe she could offer some insight into what might be going on in Cam's head.

❖

"Hi, I'm so excited we're doing this." Cindy greeted Dawn warmly.

"I'm excited too but also nervous."

"Nothing to be nervous about. Cooking isn't that hard once you know some of the basics. Don't worry, we'll get you there. Did you have some idea of what you wanted to make for Cam?"

"I'm not sure, maybe butternut squash lasagna?"

Cindy laughed gently. "Oh, honey, now you're making me nervous. That's quite a hard dish to make. We can get you there with some time, but how about something easier for a first go. Did you have a second option?"

"Um…" Dawn shrugged. "Spaghetti?"

"Perfect! We can totally work with that. I even have all the ingredients for that on hand. I love that we can do this in the middle of the day. Not many people have such flexible work schedules. Let's start with something simple. How are your vegetable chopping skills?"

"I'm decent at chopping and dicing, I do those all the time for salads."

"Great, then you're ahead of the game. Why don't you start with this onion? We'll prepare all the ingredients and then work on the process of putting it all together."

"Great. Thanks for doing this Cindy."

"No problem, I love this type of thing."

After they finished cooking, they sat to enjoy the meal. Dawn twirled pasta onto her fork and took a bite. "This is delicious."

"And not too hard to make, right?"

"It's true."

After a few moments, Dawn said, "Can I ask you a question? If it's not something you feel comfortable talking about you can totally say no."

"Go ahead and ask and then we'll see."

"It's about Cam and me."

"I thought it might be."

"So, a couple weeks ago we slept together, but it was just the one night. Since then Cam won't do anything more than kiss me. I've tried to make it clear that I'm open for more, but she always says there's no rush." Dawn shrugged. "I don't understand what she's waiting for."

"Can I ask you something?"

"You can ask me anything."

"Okay, correct me if I'm wrong, but since you've known Cam, up until a few weeks ago, hadn't you told her and maintained that you didn't do relationships?"

Dawn blushed, but her gaze never wavered from Cindy's. "Yes, that is what I said, but getting to know Cam changed things for me."

"Do you think it is possible Cam's scared you'll change your mind again?"

"I suppose anything's possible. But I won't. I'm in love with her."

"Okay, let's put that aside for a moment. The only other reason I can think of that Cam would hesitate is that she needs time to adjust to the change in your relationship."

Dawn furrowed her brow. "Do you think that's it?"

"I do know you're the first person she's felt this deeply about since Melanie died. But no, knowing Cam, I think she would have figured out what she was okay with before she started pursuing you. So me, personally, I think she's waiting on you. She needs to know you're sure about what you want before she takes it any further. I suspect if you took your relationship to the next level and then you backed away it would devastate her. I'm sure she wants and needs you to be certain. But the best advice I can give you is to ask Cam. Have a conversation with her and let her tell you what's going on with her."

"That's something to think about. Thanks for the ear."

"Any time, I'm glad you've come into Cam's life."

"I know some people may think my mind changed pretty quickly, but Cam made an impression from the first day I met her and slowly made her way into my heart. Now I can't imagine life without her."

Chapter Twenty

Dawn and Cam strolled through Balboa Park hand in hand, enjoying the beautiful summer morning. Noon was still an hour off, but the temperature had already climbed into the high seventies. All around the park, people were running, doing yoga, or playing games. Frisbees were whizzing through the air. A group playing five-a-side soccer was off to the side. Nets were set up for raucous volleyball games, young lovers cuddled together on beach blankets, moms and dads pushed strollers, and canines big and small pulled their owners toward the fenced off dog area on the edge of the grounds.

"I'm looking forward to meeting Jo and Rhonda this afternoon. Will you tell me more about them?" Dawn said.

Cam paused, thinking about where to start. "Let's see, you already know Jo went to college with us. She's a great person and has always been an amazing friend. Some of our best stories from college involve Jo and her legendary plans for pranks. She's originally from Amherst but after college, she lived here until last year when she moved back to Massachusetts to be with Rhonda. Jo went to high school with Rhonda's daughters."

"Whoa."

"I know. It seemed strange to me too at first, but I was one of the few that witnessed the night the two of them reconnected, at our friend Amy's wedding last October. I didn't have any idea that anything would come of it. But it felt right, somehow, the two of them together. Even though Jo was trying to keep her distance because she didn't think anything could happen between them. As far as Jo knew, Rhonda had never been with a woman and Jo respected her too much to make a move." Cam indicated a spot under a tree far enough away from all the ball games that neither of them would get clobbered while picnicking. "How's this?"

"Looks great."

Cam set down the picnic basket and pulled out the blanket. Dawn helped her spread it out and the two of them lay on it facing one another.

Dawn urged Cam to finish her story, "How did Jo get over that?"

"Rhonda kissed her."

Dawn laughed. "That would do it."

"Seems like it took more than one kiss for us," Cam said good-naturedly.

Dawn reached out and lifted a lock of hair off Cam's forehead. "That's only because I'm a slow learner." She leaned forward and kissed Cam tenderly. "Luckily, now we can do that any time we want."

"Amen."

Laughing, Dawn rolled onto her back and rested her head on her arm. "So then what happened?"

"The two of them decided to explore what was between them. It didn't take them long to figure it out. Kate, June, and I went to their wedding last December."

"Wonderful. So, now they're coming here to take care of Jo's condo?"

"Yeah, I figure it's mostly an excuse to come to San Diego. Jo's ex, Aideen, has been staying in the condo and Jo will probably just sell it to her. I imagine all the paperwork could have been done long distance. But it will be good to see Jo and get to know Rhonda a little better, no matter what the reason."

"You told everyone to come over around three?"

"Yep, it's a beautiful day for a cookout and I thought it would be great to have everyone hang out at the house rather than in a loud restaurant, that way we can have better quality conversations."

"I agree. So how would you like to spend the next few hours?"

"Well, everything's all set for later. We could ride up the coast again or walk around the park some more. Or did you have something else in mind?"

"You could say that." Dawn pushed Cam onto her back and rolled on top of her. She insinuated one leg between Cam's and kissed her. Teasing her lips with her tongue and then slipping her tongue into Cam's warm, sweet mouth, she savored the taste. She slid her hands up into Cam's hair and pulled her closer. When Cam moaned, she didn't stop. Instead she increased the pressure between Cam's legs.

Cam's body was on fire and she was about to lose herself. She bucked her hips and rolled, so she was now on top. She shifted a fraction of an inch away from Dawn, relieving the pressure on her throbbing clit. She slowed the kiss and lifted her head. Dawn's lips were swollen and open waiting for more. When her eyes opened, Cam noted the surprise in the green turbulent pools. She tried to add levity to the situation. "A couple more minutes and we might have given the whole park a show."

Dawn gripped Cam's shoulders and held her in place. She didn't want to let her back away this time. "So, let's go home and continue this in private."

Instead of answering, Cam kissed Dawn's forehead and rolled away. Dawn let her go. Cam sat up, pulled her knees to her chest, wrapped one arm around her knees, and clasped that wrist loosely with her other hand. She was still beside Dawn, but her gaze was fixed in the distance.

Dawn sat up and studied her profile noting the tense set of her jaw. "Cam, what's going on?"

Cam glanced briefly at Dawn and then fixed her eyes on a volleyball game off a ways. "Hmm, what do you mean?"

"You know what I mean. I just blatantly propositioned you and you put the brakes on. I want to know why. Unless I'm reading things wrong you want to be with me as much as I want to be with you. So what's the problem?"

Cam was quiet for so long, Dawn was certain she wasn't going to answer and she was quickly going from curious and frustrated to angry. Finally, Cam said, "I don't know. I mean, I don't understand it myself. I love you, and God, I do want you. You are definitely not misreading that…but for some reason I can't explain even to me, I keep stopping. I wish I knew what was happening, but I don't."

The sadness in Cam's eyes broke Dawn's heart. She scooted over so she was right next to Cam and laid her hand on her arm. "Oh, baby. I didn't know you were struggling with anything. Why didn't you say something before now? Is there anything I can do? Or anything you want to talk about?"

"I didn't know what to say. I don't even know what's going on so there's nothing I can explain. I think I just need a little more time. Is that okay?"

Dawn lifted Cam's chin, so she could look her in the eye. "It's absolutely okay, sweetheart. You take all the time you need."

Cam released a pent-up breath and leaned over and kissed Dawn softly on the lips. "Thank you. How about we finish this picnic and then go for a quick ride before everyone comes over?"

"Sounds perfect," Dawn said sincerely.

The rest of lunch was pretty subdued. They were both lost in their own thoughts. And motorcycle rides did not foster conversation. So Dawn had a long time to think about Cam's revelations. She knew Cam was turned on by her. Even this afternoon in the park, Dawn could feel Cam's arousal, yet Cam had pulled away. What was keeping her from wanting to be intimate with Dawn? That was the million-dollar question. When

Dawn had revealed she was in love with Cam, before Cam had a chance to respond, Dawn had wondered if she was too late, if Cam no longer wanted that type of relationship with her. Cam had assured her she wasn't and that she definitely still did. But… clearly something was still between the two of them, and until one or both of them figured out what that was, Dawn would keep her word and give Cam all the time she needed. It was more than fair since Cam had done the same for her when she needed time to figure things out for herself.

Cam pulled into the driveway and stopped the motorcycle. She let Dawn dismount before she followed suit. She didn't think she would ever tire of watching Dawn take off her helmet and shake out all that flaming red hair. She appeared so carefree and happy. Riding the bike, with Dawn holding on tightly behind her never failed to stir Cam up. She wished she knew why it also unsettled her now.

Dawn came close and leaned in. "That was a great ride."

Cam pulled Dawn to her.

Dawn wrapped her arms around her neck and pulled her down for a long, searing kiss. "I meant what I said before, you take all the time you need. Whenever, whatever you need, I will be right here."

"I appreciate that. I love you, Dawn."

"I love you, Cam." She stole another quick kiss. "Now let's go make sure everything's ready for our guests."

"Yes, ma'am."

Chapter Twenty-one

Cam and Dawn sat on the back patio sipping beers and talking about nothing in particular when the doorbell rang. "I'll get it," Cam said. She was surprised when she opened the door to June and Kate. "Since when do you two ring the bell?"

"Since we didn't know if we'd be interrupting something," June said with a glint in her eye.

Cam glanced down at her pants. "All zipped up. You're safe."

Kate laughed. "You can't blame us. Your relationship is still new. We're sure you don't spend a whole lot of time outside the bedroom."

"You'd be surprised."

June pretended to hold her hands over her ears. "Please don't go into all the other places you are getting busy. I don't want to know."

They all laughed and made their way out to the patio. Cam saw no reason to clue them in to how little action was actually happening. She had shared many personal things with her friends over the years, but for some reason she felt like this was something she didn't want to share with them, at least not right now. Maybe it was because the two of them were friends with Dawn as well. In any case, this was not the time to go into any details.

June and Kate greeted Dawn, then grabbed beers from the cooler and made themselves comfortable. Jack and Mozz wandered over to welcome the new arrivals and were rewarded with full body rubs.

Next to arrive were Cindy and Lynn. Kate happened to be in the kitchen when the two of them walked through the front door. She pointed to the backyard. "Everyone's out back."

Cindy held up the dish in her hands. "I'll put this potato salad in the refrigerator first."

"Yummy."

Cam went to the door again when the bell pealed a second time. As soon as she opened the door, Cam pulled Jo into a fierce hug. "It's about time."

As soon as Cam released Jo, she wrapped her arms around Rhonda tightly. "Welcome to San Diego. I'm so glad you both could come."

"Thanks, Cam. It's great to see you again," Rhonda said.

"You too. Everyone's outside. Would you like a quick tour or do you just want to jump in?"

"Oh, let's jump in. You can show us around later."

After all the introductions were handled and everyone had something to drink, Cam set out appetizer trays. She wouldn't put the steaks on right away, and she didn't want anyone drinking too much on an empty stomach.

"Dawn," Cindy said, "Since we're so close, would you mind giving us a tour of your studio?"

"I don't mind at all."

Jo said, "I'll stay here with Cam. Have fun."

Everyone else jumped at the chance to see Dawn's art.

As the others crossed the yard and passed through the gate, Jo grabbed a fresh beer and walked over to Cam where she was lighting the charcoal so the grill could get hot for the steaks. "So, you want to tell me what's going on?"

Cam turned in surprise and brushed off her hands. "What are you talking about?"

"You're in a brand new relationship which means you should be getting plenty of stress relief, so why the hell are you so tense I could break an egg on your neck?"

"How can you possibly know that?"

Jo stared at Cam waiting for an answer to her own questions.

Cam met Jo's steady gaze. "Dawn and I haven't slept together in weeks."

"What? Why not? Trouble in paradise already?"

"No, nothing like that. Things are good between us, but I keep putting the brakes on every time we get close."

"Come again. Why on earth for?"

"Dawn's made it clear that she wants to sleep with me."

"Okay…so what's the problem?"

"I love her and I want her, but I'm not sure I trust her feelings for me."

"Because until a few weeks ago she was telling you she doesn't date, that she'd basically sworn off relationships?"

"That's part of it. But something happened and I should have told her about it, but I didn't. Now, I'm thinking I don't trust her even though I want to. I'm not sure I trust that she won't change her mind if things get hard or maybe it's that I don't want her to have to deal with things if life got too hard."

"What would get hard? What's going on?"

Cam checked to make sure she and Jo had time to finish this conversation in private. "I found a lump."

"Fuck!"

"Yeah." Cam released a long, slow breath. "Exactly."

"Have you seen the doctor?"

"Yes."

"And?"

"And I'm scheduled for a mammogram the day after tomorrow."

"You haven't told anybody?"

"No."

"Why not?"

"I don't know anything yet."

"You know enough to have someone with you. Jesus, Cam! This must bring up so much. How are you keeping it all inside?"

The corners of Cam's mouth lifted in a ghost of a smile that didn't reach her eyes. "Mostly denial."

"That's not going to work forever."

"I know."

"You need to tell Dawn."

Cam stared at the ground but didn't say anything.

"She loves you, Cam. She deserves to make the decision to be with you for herself. You need to trust her, and if she doesn't deserve your trust isn't it better to find out now?"

"I guess. But I don't want to ruin what we have."

"What do you really have if you can't trust the woman you love to stand by you?"

"But it's all still so new and it took a lot for us to get here. Dawn deserves to know. You're right, I need to tell her."

"Good. You know I'm never too far away if you ever need anything, right?"

"I know. Thank you, Jo."

"One more thing before everybody gets back, if your conversation with Dawn doesn't go the way I think it will, and she doesn't insist on going with you on Monday, call me and I'll go. You shouldn't be alone for that."

Cam's throat tightened with emotion. "Okay."

By the time the others returned from the impromptu art show, Jo had Cam laughing about the latest antics of Rhonda's grandchildren. "All of them keep us on our toes and Christie delivered a beautiful little girl three weeks ago. I'll show you pictures after dinner."

"You love being surrounded by kids, don't you?" Cam said, appreciating Jo's enthusiasm.

Rhonda overheard this and chimed in as she wrapped her arm around Jo's waist. "She can't seem to get enough of them and every one of them loves her too. I think she's the favorite."

Jo kissed Rhonda quickly. "Hi, how was the art tour?"

"You missed something special. Dawn is very talented. We will definitely have to go back over there together. She has a piece I'd like for the living room."

"Sounds like a plan."

As they freshened their drinks Cam put the steaks on the grill. Dawn brought Cam a cold beer and wrapped her arms around her neck and pulled her down for a tender kiss and said low enough so only Cam could hear, "I missed you."

Cam's hands rested lightly on Dawn's hip. She put her head on Dawn's, drawing in the scent she couldn't put out of her mind. "I love you."

❖

As the flames died down in the fire pit, Lynn stood and pulled Cindy to her feet. "It's time I get this one home."

June and Kate shared a look. "We'll walk out with you," June said.

At that point everyone stood and exchanged hugs and good-byes.

Jo said, "We should probably get out of here too. We'll see you all tomorrow at the beach, right?"

There was a chorus of agreement and everyone moved en masse to the front door. Cam closed the door on the last of their guests and turned to Dawn who was by her side. "Did you have fun?"

"I had a great time. Rhonda and Jo are fantastic, and you were right when you said the two of them work. I know exactly what you mean. I'm glad we'll get to spend more time with them tomorrow."

"Me too." Cam reached for Dawn's hand. "Are you tired?"

"A little, mostly I'm relaxed but not really sleepy yet. Why?"

Cam led Dawn over to the couch and pulled her down so she was facing her. "We need to talk."

"Okay." Dawn frowned at Cam's serious tone. "Is everything okay?"

"I'm not sure. That's what I need to talk with you about."

"You're starting to worry me. What's going on? Are you okay?"

Cam held Dawn's hand in hers and ran her thumb lightly across the top as she spoke. "Something happened the other day, and I should have told you about it sooner. I'm still not sure why I didn't."

"What happened?" Dawn asked.

"I found a lump in my breast."

Dawn leaned forward, her forehead close to Cam's. She squeezed Cam's hand. "Have you been to the doctor?"

"Yeah. She's sending me for a mammogram on Monday."

"What time? I'm going with you."

Cam's eyes opened wide. "You are?"

"Of course I am. Did you think I wouldn't?"

"I didn't know what to think. I know it's a lot. We haven't been dating that long. If you don't want to go, I'd understand."

"Seriously? You're not going alone and I want to be there with and for you. Wait, is this why you didn't tell me? Did you think I'd run if things got tough?"

Cam didn't miss the flash of hurt in Dawn's eyes. She shrugged. "Maybe I thought it was too much too soon. I know how hard it is being on your side of things."

"All the more reason for me to go with you. This must bring up so much for you. You've got to be thinking about Melanie."

"Some."

"No doubt. Who have you told?" Dawn asked.

"Only you and Jo, but she figured out something was wrong on her own."

"I should have too. I'm sorry I didn't." Dawn rubbed Cam's leg. "Listen, I know you're not ready for sex, and I respect that, but…I would like to stay tonight. Would it be okay if we just sleep together?"

Cam was absolutely sure that wasn't the best idea, but she wanted to hold Dawn too. "I would like that."

Dawn borrowed a T-shirt and used a new toothbrush Cam had on hand. By the time she finished changing in the bathroom, Cam had stripped down to a T-shirt and boxer briefs.

Cam looked over when the bathroom door opened. Her T-shirt fell to the middle of Dawn's thighs. Her gaze lingered on Dawn's long, creamy white legs. Her red hair tumbled past her shoulders. Cam wanted to run her fingers through it and pull Dawn close and breathe her in. Her clit twitched with lust, so she did the most logical thing she could think to do, she escaped to the bathroom to brush her teeth. As she moved past Dawn on her way, Dawn stopped her with a hand to her arm, and Cam's mouth went dry.

"Which side of the bed do you sleep on when you're actually sleeping?"

Cam could barely breathe. "Um…usually the right but either side is fine."

"Perfect, I sleep on the left."

Before Cam could make a complete fool of herself, she made a hasty exit.

By the time she returned, Dawn had slid under the covers. She was still alluring, but Cam almost had a handle on her desire. She could just give in and make love with Dawn. She knew without a doubt Dawn was willing, but it still didn't feel right. She wished she knew what was wrong with her, and she wasn't thinking about the potential health issues. There was a beautiful woman in her bed, and she wasn't planning on having sex with her tonight.

"You okay?"

"Hmm, yeah, why?"

"You're standing in the middle of the floor looking at me in your bed like we're going to swallow you whole if you come any closer."

Cam laughed at herself. "Yeah, I was standing here telling myself how crazy it is that I don't plan to have sex tonight with the gorgeous woman in my bed."

Dawn absently licked her lips. "Either way is fine with me, but the choice is yours. I meant it when I said I just want to hold you tonight."

"I know you did. I'm just having a hard time figuring out why I'm not ready for more than that."

Dawn patted the bed beside her. "Come over here. I promise I won't bite until you want me to."

Cam swallowed hard and climbed into bed next to Dawn, careful not to touch her quite yet. She lay on her back and pulled the covers over her chest. Dawn scooted down in the bed and rolled toward Cam. She laid her head on Cam's shoulder and put her hand on Cam's stomach, stroking softly. When Cam's muscles tightened under her light touch, she stilled her hand and met Cam's eyes. "Sorry."

Cam laid her hand on top of Dawn's. "No, it's okay. You know I want you and I do, badly."

"I do know. Your body tells me that very clearly whenever we touch. But I don't want us to make love again until you're ready. Until your body, head, and heart are on the same page, I don't want you to have any regrets."

Cam lifted her head and kissed the top of Dawn's head. "Thank you."

"I love you, Cam."

"I love you, too. Roll over so I can spoon with you."

Dawn complied and Cam wrapped her body around Dawn's. Dawn breathed deeply, trying to ease the sudden tension in her body. She had promised Cam that she could set the pace so she would resist seducing her, no matter how much she wanted to. Tonight was about comforting her and just being together. As their bodies fit snugly together, Cam melted into the comfort. She wrapped her right arm over Dawn's breasts. Dawn held Cam's arm with her own, binding them tightly together. After a few minutes of silence, Dawn asked, "Are you scared?"

"Some, I guess. Mostly I'm trying to remember I don't know anything yet, so there's nothing to be afraid of yet."

Dawn stroked Cam's forearm that she held to her chest. "I hope there is nothing to worry about even when we do know more. But no matter what we find out on Monday, I'm going to be with you every step of the way."

Cam closed her eyes, absorbing the words into her soul. "Thank you." She squeezed Dawn tightly. "Will you tell me about your parents' farm so I can think about something else and maybe I can sleep?"

"Happily," Dawn said. She told Cam stories about the farm, the animals, and her parents until Cam fell asleep. The pit of fear that had planted itself in her stomach as soon as Cam told her about the lump reared its ugly head and she shivered. She wasn't going to lose Cam now, she couldn't. *God, Cam can't be sick. Please, she just can't be.* Dawn closed her eyes and willed herself to sleep.

Cam awoke with a start. She loved waking up with Dawn wrapped in her arms. Dawn's scent sent her body spiraling upward again. She needed to get out of here now while she still could. She eased out of bed, pulled on her jeans, and wandered into the kitchen to make coffee. Her body was almost under control when Dawn stumbled out looking all tousled and beautiful.

Dawn smiled when she saw Cam in the kitchen. "Hey, good lookin'."

"Good morning. How did you sleep?"

"Good, but I missed you when you weren't there when I woke up."

"Yeah, uh, I…"

Once she was close enough, Dawn put her hands on Cam's cheeks and made her meet her gaze. "I understand. I felt the same way while you were holding me last night." She pulled Cam down for a tender kiss and kept it light. Then she moved her hands to Cam's shoulders. "Hell, I'm still turned on, I won't lie, but the next move is yours, baby. You don't have to run or hide it from me. I'm glad being close to me turns you on."

Cam laid her chin on Dawn's head and held her close. "Sweetheart, you don't have to be anywhere nearby to get me hot. All I have to do is think about you. This morning I felt like my body was going to explode and you weren't even awake."

Dawn stroked Cam's chest gently, aiming to soothe not arouse. "Do you have any clearer of an idea why you aren't ready yet?"

You mean like the fact that I'm scared that I feel too much for you. The last time we slept together, you ran away. Of course there were mitigating factors, but still, that doesn't do a lot for a person's confidence. You've said you love me, and I feel that from you, but part of me still wonders when you'll change your mind again. "I think I'm getting closer to figuring it out, but I'm not quite ready to talk about it yet. Is that okay?"

"You know it is." Dawn stood on her tiptoes to place another light kiss on Cam's lips. "Now can I have a cup of that amazing-smelling coffee?"

"Coming right up."

❖

Dawn felt like it would be easier for Cam if she showered at her own place, so after breakfast, she dressed in the clothes she'd worn yesterday and made plans with Cam to meet back up to go to the beach with their friends that afternoon. Now, as she stood in the shower, she couldn't stop thinking about how it felt to share a bed with Cam. To be held so close. She knew Cam hadn't snuggled her as tightly as she might have and she knew why. She wished she could somehow put Cam at ease with the thought of making love with her.

It bothered her immensely that Cam had not told her about the lump as soon as she found it. But that was nothing compared to what Cam must be going through. She would just have to show Cam that she meant what she said, that she would be there for her every step of the way, no matter what happened. After the shower, she was still stirred up. Emotion and lust swirling through her, there was only one safe place for her to put all of the feeling. So, after pulling on some loose clothes, she made her way into the studio and placed a fresh canvas on an easel and put all the tumultuous passion into the painting.

CHAPTER TWENTY-TWO

Once Dawn left, Cam went into her bedroom, changed into workout clothes, and headed out to the patio after feeding the dogs. She donned her boxing gloves and spent the next thirty minutes working the heavy bag. The session helped ease some of her frustration, but the persistent ache between her thighs was still very present. She went inside and headed for the shower. She stood under the hot spray letting the cascading water work on her tense muscles. She briefly considered taking care of the arousal that still gripped her groin, but the thought of getting herself off left her hollow. She twisted off the faucets, quickly dried herself, and pulled on clothes.

She grabbed her keys and helmet and roared down the driveway on her bike. No destination in mind. She had to get a little distance to be able to think. Dawn had said she'd see her later, and Cam knew she wouldn't come over before then, but just knowing Dawn was next door made thinking about her and their situation hard.

Rather than head for the coast, she steered the bike toward the mountains. It didn't take her long to figure out where her heart was leading her. She drove for more than an hour, through Alpine. She climbed higher, up the winding road of the Sunrise Highway, to the far end of the Cleveland National Forest. Just past the Mount Laguna Lodge, she slowed and turned left then took an almost immediate right into a small parking lot. She left the bike and easily found the trailhead. She hiked to the top of the path, sat on the large boulder at the top, and surveyed the stunning view.

Tears formed in her eyes, clouding her vision. She took a deep breath. This was the spot she had spread Melanie's ashes two years before. She had been back a couple of times when she needed or wanted to feel especially close to Mel. The two of them had spent numerous vacations down at the Lodge and had always hiked this path, often packing a picnic lunch to share while taking in the scenery. A lump formed in her throat. She wasn't saying good-bye to Melanie again. She didn't need to do that. Deep down Mel would always be a part of her and Dawn knew it too and understood and accepted the fact. But she wasn't likely to come back here, at least not alone.

So, with a mixture of sad and happy tears, she started talking aloud as though Melanie could hear her. She told her all about Dawn, without leaving out a single step of their relationship. Then she told her about the lump and how scared she was that she would become a burden to Dawn because she loved her so much. She talked and cried herself out. She scrubbed her face dry then laughed at herself, thinking about what Melanie would say if she came across her like this.

The experience was cathartic. She descended the path with a sense of peace infusing her entire being. She swung her leg over the bike, pulled her helmet on, and began the journey home. On the way back, she was able to think much more positively about a future with Dawn. She had only said good-bye to her a couple of hours ago, but she couldn't wait to see her. As Cam pulled into her driveway, Dawn was just crossing the yard between their homes. She greeted Cam with a friendly wave. Cam turned off the engine and removed her helmet. "Hi, babe."

"Hi," Dawn said. She stepped to Cam as she climbed off the bike. She lifted her hand to Cam's cheek and stroked. "What's going on? Have you been crying?"

Cam put her hands lightly on Dawn's hips and pulled her close. She dipped her head for a quick kiss because she couldn't help herself. "I have. Come inside while I change and I'll tell you all about it."

Dawn sat on the bed as Cam changed in the bathroom with the door ajar so she could talk to Dawn. She told Dawn all about her trip. She told her about the significance of the spot, about talking to Melanie, and everything. "I didn't know that's where I was headed when I left this morning. I just needed a little distance to think and just knowing you were next door was pretty distracting."

"I get that. You're pretty distracting yourself." She stayed where she was and Cam sat beside her. "The place you went, where you spread Melanie's ashes, it sounds like an amazing spot."

Cam took Dawn's hand in hers and met her eyes. "It is. I'd like to take you there some time."

Dawn squeezed Cam's hand and didn't let go. "I'd love to see it someday."

"Okay, then. In the meantime we have friends to meet at the beach. Should we take the truck so we can take beach chairs?"

"Well, since June and Lynn both said they'd bring coolers, if we just take a blanket and towels, we can take the bike and it will be easier to find parking."

"Sounds like a plan."

Dawn hadn't missed that the spark was a little brighter in Cam's eyes when she returned from her trip to the mountains. Clearly it had been good for her. As she sat behind her on the bike, holding her tightly, she hoped Cam would continue to let her in.

❖

Cam and Dawn were the last to arrive. Their friends had already claimed a nice spot on the beach around one of the bonfire pits with chairs, umbrellas, blankets, and coolers. The two of them had barely settled onto their own blanket when June roped Cam into filling out the side in a volleyball game with her, Kate, and Jo. After a quick kiss for Dawn, Cam stood and headed for the net. Soon, Cindy convinced Lynn to walk down the beach with her and Dawn quickly found herself alone with Rhonda. Keeping an eye on the game, she moved over and dropped in the chair next to her. "How's your trip been so far?"

"Wonderful. I love San Diego and it's been so nice to get to know some of Jo's friends a bit more and meet new ones."

"It's been great getting to know you too."

"Well, in that case, I know we practically just met, but I can be a pretty good listener."

"Is it that obvious?"

"I can see the worry on your face every time you look at Cam, if that's what you mean."

"Did Jo fill you in?"

"Yes," Rhonda said gently.

"Ah. Yes, well, I don't mind telling you I'm scared. Not only scared for Cam but also of losing her."

"I can't tell you not to be because none of us knows if there's reason to be yet. But if you don't mind a little unsolicited advice…"

"By all means," Dawn said.

"Don't hide your fear from Cam."

Dawn shook her head. "I can't burden her with what I'm feeling when she already has so much going on."

"I know it seems that way. But if things had worked out differently, I might have lost Jo because I was afraid to tell her how I was really feeling. Trust me, the best course is open and honest communication with full disclosure. You've already acknowledged your love for one another. What's the point of hiding any of your other feelings?"

Dawn thought that over. "No point at all." She watched Cam stretch out her whole body as she dove for the ball and hit it up to June. Then she turned back to Rhonda. "Thanks for the ear."

"Any time."

When the game was over, June and Kate headed straight for the water, and Cam and Jo made their way back over to the chairs. Jo dusted herself off and dropped into the chair on the other side of Rhonda. Cam stood slightly away so as not to get sand on the blankets. Jo said, "You two should come out this fall and stay with us. Fall foliage is beautiful and we have plenty of room."

Cam shared a look with Dawn before she responded. "That sounds like a lot of fun. We'll talk about it. For now, though, I'm going to steal my girlfriend away if I can convince her to take a dip with me. I need to cool down."

Dawn stood and walked to Cam. "I thought you'd never ask." Jo and Rhonda's laughter followed them down to the water. As Dawn walked with Cam, their hands entwined, she said, "You do realize being in the water with you will do nothing to cool me off. It will just make me so hot for you everyone around us will know what I'm thinking."

"Then that makes two of us. Come with me anyway."

"I'll come with you anywhere, anytime, my love."

Cam laughed heartily. "Now that's just plain sexy."

Dawn pulled Cam into the ocean. "It's just plain true. You remember it."

"How could I possibly forget?"

The rest of the afternoon passed pleasantly as they sat around swapping stories, taking walks along the shoreline, and taking dips in the ocean.

When everyone started getting hungry, Cam and Jo took burrito orders and went to a nearby taquería to get dinner. As Jo pulled the rental car out of the parking lot, without any preamble, she said, "You told her."

"I did. How'd you know?"

Jo shrugged. "There's more of an…easiness between the two of you today that wasn't there yesterday. Given that, I take it I was right."

"Yes, she said she was going with me. I know she was hurt that I didn't tell her right away, but she didn't say anything about that, just that she'd be with me every step of the way."

"And you're not sure you're happy about that because you know how hard that could end up being, but it does make you happy that she loves you enough to offer that."

"When did you become a mind reader?"

"You've never been hard to figure out, my friend."

"Well, you're right. It does make me happy that she wants to be there for me, but I don't want to be a burden on her. Our relationship is still so new…"

"I'm only going to ask this one time and before you answer, remember I know what you're thinking. If the situation was reversed would you listen to her if she told you to go away because it was too much and you didn't need to hold her hand?"

Cam didn't even think before she answered. "Of course not, I'd think life was unfair, again. But I would be by her side to fight whatever fight she needed to win."

"Right." Jo didn't say anything more. She just let Cam sit with that thought for several minutes. "So what makes you think she would turn away from you even if you told her to?"

Cam didn't answer. She didn't need to. Jo had made her point and both of them knew it.

After getting the burritos, Cam and Jo headed back. Jo asked, "So, when are you planning on telling the others?"

"I was thinking maybe after dinner while we're all together so I only have to say it once more. But I didn't want to put a shadow on the whole day."

Chapter Twenty-three

Dawn let herself into Cam's house at quarter to seven on Monday morning. She had decided to sleep at her own place the night before, thinking Cam would be more comfortable that way. She heard the shower running, so she went into the kitchen and brewed a pot of coffee. She had just poured two cups and was doctoring her own when Cam walked into the kitchen. She wore her usual workday clothes of slacks and a button-down shirt. "Good morning, sweetheart."

Dawn slid the cup of black coffee over the counter to Cam. "Good morning. Did you sleep?"

"Some."

"Understandable. I thought about toasting bagels, but I didn't know if you'd be up for eating."

"I'm not."

Dawn moved around the island and wrapped her arms around Cam's waist. She laid her head on her shoulder. "Why don't you call in sick? Then after the appointment, we can have breakfast or go for a walk in the park or something."

"I took the morning off. We can do those things before I head to the office."

"Good. Are you ready to go?"

"Yeah. Thanks for going with me."

"No thanks needed. I love you, Cam. I need to know what we're facing. Besides, it will help to have someone else hearing what the doctor says today."

Cam kissed Dawn deeply. "I love you, too."

❖

Dawn wasn't sure what the protocol was for this type of thing. She'd never accompanied anyone to a doctor's appointment before. Was she allowed to go back with Cam? Would Cam even want her to? Cam was staring into space. She squeezed the hand she was holding to get Cam's attention. "Nervous?"

The corners of Cam's mouth turned up in a small grin. "I'd be lying if I said I wasn't. But it helps that you're here."

Before Dawn could respond, the door next to the check-in desk opened and a nurse called Cam's name. Cam stood, but before she moved forward, she held out her hand to Dawn. "Coming?"

Dawn stood and took Cam's hand. "Anywhere, anytime, any reason."

The response made Cam smile which lifted Dawn's heart. She stood outside the changing room after the nurse gave Cam instructions and then walked with Cam to the second waiting room after she had taken off the top half of her clothes and exchanged them for a gown. Seeing Cam in a hospital gown made it more real for Dawn, and she reached for Cam's hand both to comfort and be comforted. "You really do look sexy in anything you wear." There was a snicker from a woman across the room, but Dawn held Cam's gaze.

"I could say the same. When you're gardening and you're covered from head to toe to protect your skin from the sun, you're as sexy as you were in that bikini yesterday."

Dawn laughed. "Thanks, by the way, for reapplying that sun block so often."

"My pleasure." Cam's smile reached her eyes this time.

"Cameron."

Cam and Dawn turned to the nurse who had entered the waiting room unnoticed by either of them. Dawn stood with Cam this time and held her hand on the way in.

The mammogram itself was uncomfortable but relatively painless. Cam appreciated that Dawn kept up a steady stream of dialogue with her and the technician. Once the images were taken, Cam and Dawn were ushered into another exam room where Cam was instructed to lie on the exam table and another technician would be in shortly for the ultrasound.

Alone again with Cam, Dawn said, "The doctor seems to have ordered the whole gamut of tests."

Cam caught the hint of apprehension in Dawn's voice. "It doesn't necessarily mean anything is wrong. I'm sure she just wants to have as much information as possible before giving me her opinion."

"I'm sure you're right." Nevertheless, Dawn moved closer and clasped Cam's hand in her own.

❖

An hour later, Dawn and Cam sat at a table in Snooze, one of their favorite places for breakfast in Hillcrest. The smell of coffee, cinnamon, and maple syrup hung heavy in the air. The clatter of flatware and murmured conversations filled their ears. "This feels a bit surreal," Dawn said.

"I know. Once we left the radiology building, it's just felt like a normal day. But it's not."

Dawn reached over and put her hand on Cam's. "It's not, but whatever happens, we're in this together."

Cam turned her hand up and Dawn's fingers easily entwined with hers. "Dawn, I would understand if this is too much. I wouldn't blame you if you walked away."

Dawn remembered where she was just in time to modify her tone from the angry outrage she'd been about to unleash. "Don't ever say that to me again. Don't dismiss me. Do you really think so little of me, of us? What the hell, Cam?"

Cam shrugged and looked at their hands still linked on the table. "You have a choice."

"I already made my choice. I chose you. I will continue to choose you for as long as you want me. So if this is too hard for you and you don't want me around then you need to tell me that now. If you don't want me, that is the one and only reason I would leave, now or ever."

Cam studied Dawn. She saw only resolve, no hint of doubt in her beautiful features. "I want you. I will want you forever."

Dawn squeezed the hand she still held. "Well, that's good then. This should work out fine. I'm glad we had this little chat."

Cam chuckled in relief. "I love you."

Dawn's eyes softened and her lips twitched upward. "I love you too, you crazy woman."

After their breakfast arrived, Dawn asked, "So, what are the next steps?"

Cam thought for a minute. "Well, sometimes the scans make it clear there's nothing to worry about. But if the doctor can't tell with certainty nothing is wrong, she'll want to do a biopsy."

"How soon will we know?"

Cam's phone, sitting on the table, trilled at that exact moment. They studied it warily. Finally, Cam picked it up and her eyes locked on Dawn's, her face draining of color as the conversation progressed. "Hello…Yes…Okay…I can make that work…Thank you…See you then…Bye." Cam hung up the phone. "I'm scheduled for a biopsy tomorrow morning."

Before Dawn said anything, she grabbed some bills from her wallet and threw them on the table. Then she stood and held her hand out to Cam. "Let's get out of here."

Cam took Dawn's hand and let herself be led outside. Dawn steered them down the street, toward the car. "Tell me."

Cam cleared her throat. "The scans aren't clear and she wants to get answers as quickly as possible. If it's malignant she wants to set a treatment plan and start right away."

"Okay, that's what she's said from the beginning, right? Nothing new, this is just the next step. What time do we need to be at the hospital in the morning?"

"Five."

"Okay." Dawn gripped Cam's hand tightly in hers as the park came into view. "Are you still planning to go in to work today?"

Cam stared off into the distance. "Yeah, I should. I'll have to take the rest of the week off or at least work from home the couple days after surgery. I need to go in and arrange that. Plus if I keep busy there, maybe I can keep my mind off this for a little while."

"Makes sense. Let's head back to the car so you can drop me off at the house before you head in."

"Sure."

❖

Cam was still in a daze. She had hoped the scans would reveal the lump was something inconsequential. Now she had to have a biopsy. Tomorrow. Everything was happening so fast. The only thing keeping her going was Dawn. She was steady. She was scared too, Cam could see it. But she was also certain Dawn would see this through to the end, whichever way it went. That was a comfort even if she felt selfish for needing it. After making the arrangements she needed to at work, Cam closed herself in her office and tried to get her desk cleared off.

Her desire to be productive kept being interrupted by memories of Mel and her fight with cancer. It was an insidious disease. Mel had been young and healthy before her diagnosis. What were her own odds? She reflected on what Dawn had said at breakfast, and while she appreciated it, she still felt selfish that she might put her through the same thing she herself had lived through with Melanie.

She loved Dawn. That was fact. She loved her differently than she'd loved Melanie. Perhaps even deeper because of the experience she'd gained in the years with her. She would never minimize what she'd shared with Mel, and she didn't believe Dawn would ever ask her to. Fortunately, Dawn was with her, she loved her, and no matter what happened after tomorrow, Cam could never be sorry for that.

Chapter Twenty-four

Dawn was in Cam's kitchen making sandwiches. She had insisted Cam stay in the living room. A rare summer storm raged outside. Cam lounged on the sofa with her feet up watching a baseball game. The San Diego Padres were playing the Mariners in Seattle where ironically the weather was beautifully clear. Jack and Mozz dozed on the floor by her side. "Do you want mayo or mustard?" Dawn asked from the kitchen.

"On ham? Mustard. Always mustard."

"Coming right up."

Dawn didn't know how Cam looked so sexy sitting in shorts and a T-shirt watching TV. She tamped down her rising arousal. Cam was in no condition for either of them to even consider the idea of close contact. She'd just had a biopsy two days ago and was still extremely tender at the incision site, but that didn't stop Dawn from looking and imagining what it would be like when she was finally able to get Cam in her arms again.

"Here you go," she said handing Cam a plate with a ham and cheese sandwich and wavy potato chips.

"Thank you."

"You're welcome." Dawn set down a glass of water on the table behind the couch, easy for Cam to reach when she needed it. Then she returned to the kitchen for her own plate before heading to the chair next to the couch.

"Sit with me," Cam said, pulling her feet towards her so Dawn had room at the end of the couch.

Dawn sat crossed-legged on the couch facing Cam and bit into her sandwich. Cam hadn't yet tried the sandwich. "Is everything okay? Do you need something else?"

"I need you."

"Well, I need you too, but for right now you have to settle for the sandwich. I am not going to touch you while you're in pain."

"We can be careful."

Dawn threw her head back and laughed. "There is absolutely no way, especially based on previous experience, you can guarantee that we would be able to manage to go slow or take it easy. I'm not going to risk you pulling out your stitches and delaying what we both want any longer than necessary."

When Cam only stared back at Dawn with desire in her eyes, Dawn turned her body so she was facing the TV. "Stop looking at me like that and eat your sandwich. If you're good, after we eat we can try to cuddle if it doesn't hurt you, but you have to promise to be honest about that."

"Okay. If that's all that's on the table, I'll take it." Finally, she bit into her sandwich and turned her attention back to the game.

A couple of hours later, the Padres were losing badly to the Mariners and Cam was flipping through channels trying to find something more entertaining to watch. Dawn sat at the end of the couch again, only this time she held her sketch book and studied Cam before putting her pencil to paper. When Cam's phone rang, she stiffened perceptibly and turned to Dawn with dread. Dawn put down her pad and scooted closer to Cam who muted the TV. Dawn took Cam's hand as she answered. "Hello…Yes…Hi, Doctor…I understand," Cam said flatly.

Dawn could not hear what the doctor was saying. She could only watch Cam's face, and she wasn't giving anything away.

"I do, I understand…Thank you…I will…Bye." Cam hung up and put the phone carefully down on the end table. Then she turned to Dawn.

She squeezed Cam's hand. She wouldn't back down from whatever needed to be faced.

Cam's face lit up with a huge grin that reached her eyes. "It's benign."

Dawn had never heard sweeter words. "She's sure?"

"One hundred percent positive, she said."

"Oh, Cam!"

"She wants me to start getting annual mammograms, but otherwise I'm clear."

"Thank God. That's such a relief. We should let everyone know."

"We will, in a few minutes. First, I think I need a hug. It hasn't quite sunk in and I need some time."

Dawn laid her head on Cam's shoulder, wrapped her arms around her, and held on tightly. "I'm sure it won't for a while."

A few days later, Dawn finished prepping the last ingredient. She checked the time. It took longer than she expected, but she had been careful to make sure she did it right. She cleaned her knife and everything else she could, all the ingredients were set out on the counter waiting to be put together. She and Cindy had met several times and made a number of dishes, but Dawn decided sticking with spaghetti for this first venture on her own was the safest bet.

After the kitchen was back in order, she made sure to set the alarm so she wouldn't forget to put dinner together before Cam left work. Then she went into the studio to finish her second surprise for Cam and started putting things in order. The plan was already fully formed. She simply needed to implement it.

When the alarm went off several hours later, she gave everything one last look, making sure everything was set and went back into the kitchen. She turned down the sauce. It smelled wonderful. She pulled out a small spoon and sampled, it tasted as great as it smelled. She'd followed Cindy's instructions exactly. She cleaned up as much as she could and went into the bedroom to change.

Dawn's phone rang just as she finished changing. She glanced at the screen. "Hi, honey, how was your day?"

"My day was good. Yours?" Cam said.

"Fun actually. Are you headed home?"

"Yes, have you thought about what you want to do for dinner?"

"Hmmm, some. Just come on over after you feed the boys. Okay?"

"Okay. See you soon."

Dawn hung up and took a deep breath. *Show time.* She opened the bottle of red wine and poured two glasses.

By the time Cam pulled into the driveway next door, Dawn was nervous. She wanted this to be a special night. The sight of Cam calmed her. Being with Cam was special all by itself. She took another calming breath and lit the candles on the table.

Dawn turned with a wine glass in hand when she heard Cam's knock on the back door. She smiled when Cam stepped into the kitchen. "Hi." She handed Cam the glass of wine.

"Thank you. What's all this? It smells delicious."

"I wanted to surprise you."

Cam moved to Dawn. "You succeeded." She leaned down for a long, slow kiss. "Hmm, I've thought about that all day."

"Me too."

"You don't cook," Cam said apprehensively.

"Cindy's been teaching me to cook."

"Seriously?"

"Yes, I told her I wanted to surprise you, so she's been giving me secret lessons since we went over there for dinner a couple weeks ago."

"You're amazing."

"Let's see how it tastes before you say that," Dawn replied with laughter in her voice.

"I'm sure it will be great, but either way you're amazing for doing this. Thank you."

"You're welcome. Shall we eat?"

"Definitely, what can I do?"

"You can pull the salad out of the fridge."

While Cam took the bowl to the table, Dawn pulled the bread out of the oven and put the pasta in the boiling water. Before joining Cam at the table, she drained the pasta and mixed it into the sauce. Cam reached for Dawn's hand. "I love you."

Dawn linked her fingers with Cam's. "I will never get tired of hearing that. I love you, too."

As they ate, Dawn asked, "Everything go okay at the clinic today?"

Cam nodded. "I was in and out in less than ten minutes. It feels so much better to have the stitches out."

"I would imagine. Does it still hurt?"

"No, not at all."

"That's fantastic."

"This is what's fantastic," Cam said, lifting a bite of spaghetti on her fork.

"I'm glad you like it."

"I love it."

"Then we'll have to remember to thank Cindy."

When dinner was done, Cam offered to clean up. Dawn pitched in and everything was taken care of quickly.

As she closed the dishwasher, Dawn turned to Cam. She pulled her down for a long kiss and she turned up the heat. She heard Cam moan, but as she anticipated, moments later, Cam lifted her head and broke the kiss.

Dawn saw the need swirling in Cam's eyes. "Baby, the other day you said you needed me. I thought you were ready. Am I wrong?"

"No. I am ready. More than ready, I want to be with you so badly. But…."

"What is it, baby?"

"Dawn…" Cam swallowed over the lump of desire in her throat and tried again. "I want…I need you to be sure. I don't want to rush you. I don't want you to have any regrets. If we take the next step there is no going back. It means we're both all in."

Dawn's smile lit her eyes and she placed her hand on Cam's cheek. "Darling, you have never, ever rushed me. I am all in. You waited patiently for me to figure out what I needed to, and I appreciate that. But I'm ready. Look at me, hear what I'm saying. You've always been able to see what I'm feeling. I love you and that won't change. I want to be with you in every way. I want to feel all of you. Wait, before you say anything I need to show you something." Dawn took Cam by the hand and led her into the studio.

Cam's heart raced and her body was on fire. She tried to clear her head to pay attention to what Dawn wanted to show her. Dawn gestured to a painting just inside the door on the left. Cam recognized the picture full of grief and anguish she saw before.

"Cam, you were the first person to see this painting. That day you fixed my computer, I'd just pulled it out from behind a stack of other paintings. I hadn't been ready for anyone else to see it, and I was trying to decide if I should include it in the show. The emotion I saw when you looked at the piece helped me make my decision. This is the first thing I painted after I left Lori. Knowing you could see what I felt when I painted it, somehow made it easier for me to let other people see it. I'm not sure I'm making a lot of sense. But this painting is only one in a whole series I did as I healed. They represent the different stages of grief when dealing with the end of my relationship with Lori." Dawn indicated a painting at the end of the row. "What do you see when you look at this painting?"

Cam studied the picture before her. "Peace."

"Exactly right, the last stage of the grief process. I wasn't able to paint this one until you came into my life. Being around you made me reevaluate everything about my life, past, present, and what I want for my future. I've been working on myself a long time. You're the first person that I care knows that. But there is another series of paintings I just finished. I think they are more important to the current conversation."

Dawn walked around to the far end of the studio where her most recent pieces were set. "This is a series of pictures I've worked on since we met. Some are still in the sketch stage, but these are my works in progress. I want you to see them now because I think the sum of them reflects and documents the progression of my feelings for you. I know you wonder if I need more time. I'm curious what you'll think after you see these paintings. Here's what I'd like to do, I want to leave you here. I want you to take your time, as much time as you need with them. Then when you're done, I want you to come find me. Okay?"

Cam nodded. "Okay, if that's what you want."

Dawn kissed Cam on the cheek. "It is exactly what I want. Come find me when you're ready."

Cam watched Dawn walk out of the room before turning her concentration to the pictures Dawn indicated. It appeared Dawn arranged the series sequentially. The first painting was a scene from the first day she and Dawn met. The two of them, June, and Kate in Cam's backyard sat around the table with pizza and wine, at first glance a portrait of celebration. Then Cam stepped closer and studied the expression on Dawn's face. *She's apprehensive.* Not all of the pieces had people. Some were of spots that were special to their budding relationship. She studied each of the sketches and canvases. She saw Dawn's fear and resistance, the heat of their first kiss, the beginnings of trust and acceptance of friendship, comfortable companionship, and affection. Dawn seemed to have documented every significant event since meeting her. Then Cam stopped. The painting Cam stood in front of was one of her and Dawn in her backyard. The dogs lazed in the sun. Dawn appeared to have just paused from weeding, and Cam was captured in the act of digging a hole. The look on Dawn's face made Cam's heart race. *This must be the day Dawn told me her story.* Cam could easily see the love reflected in Dawn's eyes. Cam let her gaze fall on the next picture and the next, viewing her relationship with Dawn through Dawn's own eyes. Clearly, Dawn put a great deal of thought and feeling into figuring out what was between the two of them. Cam's love for Dawn deepened. She hadn't known it was possible.

Cam arrived at the last easel and paused. She couldn't see the picture that Dawn covered with a cloth. Pinned to the cloth was an envelope with Cam's name on it. She removed the envelope and took out the note.

Cam, my darling,

I know what is in my heart, and I love you more than I have ever loved another. I want you in ways I never imagined. After you look at this last picture, please come to me and let me show you how much I crave your touch.

Love always,
Dawn
P.S. This painting is for your eyes only.

As Cam reached to move the cloth, she swallowed hard. She removed the cloth and couldn't move. Dawn's last painting was a self-portrait in the nude. She lay on her bed waiting for her lover to arrive. Cam's heart pounded as she hurried to find Dawn.

She found her in the bedroom, soft music playing in the background. Dawn wore nothing but a silky robe. She stood at the back window, staring out at her gardens, lost in thought.

With the sound of Cam's whispered, "Dawn?" she turned smiling and moved to Cam.

She reached out her hand, and when Cam took it she led her to the bed. She sat beside Cam on the side of the bed. "Hi, gorgeous, how was your journey down memory lane?"

"It was certainly enlightening."

"Excellent. That's exactly what I hoped it would be. Do you have any questions?"

Cam shook her head slowly. "No questions." She leaned over and kissed Dawn. This time she didn't stop.

The End

About the Author

TJ Thomas lives in western Massachusetts where she enjoys a quiet life with her college professor wyf, Elle, and their animals. TJ's passion is writing, and she spends much of her free time in that pursuit. TJ and Elle are equidistant from their two adult children who live in London and San Diego, and they enjoy traveling to all points in between and beyond.

Books Available from Bold Strokes Books

A Date to Die by Anne Laughlin. Someone is killing people close to Detective Kay Adler, who must look to her own troubled past for a suspect. There she finds more than one person seeking revenge against her. (978-1-63555-023-8)

Captured Soul by Laydin Michaels. Can Kadence Munroe save the woman she loves from a twisted killer, or will she lose her to a collector of souls? (978-1-62639-915-0)

Dawn's New Day by TJ Thomas. Can Dawn Oliver and Cam Cooper, two women who have loved and lost, open their hearts to love again? (978-1-63555-072-6)

Definite Possibility by Maggie Cummings. Sam Miller is just out for good times, but Lucy Weston makes her realize happily ever after is a definite possibility. (978-1-62639-909-9)

Eyes Like Those by Melissa Brayden. Isabel Chase and Taylor Andrews struggle between love and ambition from the writers' room on one of Hollywood's hottest TV shows. (978-1-63555-012-2)

Heart's Orders by Jaycie Morrison. Helen Tucker and Tee Owens escape hardscrabble lives to careers in the Women's Army Corps, but more than their hearts are at risk as friendship blossoms into love. (978-1-63555-073-3)

Hiding Out by Kay Bigelow. Treat Dandridge is unaware that her life is in danger from the murderer who is hunting the woman she's falling in love with, Mickey Heiden. (978-1-62639-983-9)

Omnipotence Enough by Sophia Kell Hagin. Can the tiny tool that abducted war veteran Jamie Gwynmorgan accidentally acquires help her escape an unknown enemy to reclaim her stolen life and the woman she deeply loves? (978-1-63555-037-5)

Summer's Cove by Aurora Rey. Emerson Lange moved to Provincetown to live in the moment, but when she meets Darcy Belo and her son Liam, her quest for summer romance becomes a family affair. (978-1-62639-971-6)

The Road to Wings by Julie Tizard. Lieutenant Casey Tompkins, air force student pilot, has to fly with the toughest instructor, Captain Kathryn "Hard Ass" Hardesty, fly a supersonic jet, and deal with a growing forbidden attraction. (978-1-62639-988-4)

Beauty and the Boss by Ali Vali. Ellis Renois is at the top of the fashion world, but she never expects her summer assistant Charlotte Hamner to tear her heart and her business apart like sharp scissors through cheap material. (978-1-62639-919-8)

Fury's Choice by Brey Willows. When gods walk amongst humans, can two women find a balance between love and faith? (978-1-62639-869-6)

Lessons in Desire by MJ Williamz. Can a summer love stand a four-month hiatus and still burn hot? (978-1-63555-019-1)

Lightning Chasers by Cass Sellars. For Sydney and Parker, being a couple was never what they had planned. Now they have to fight corruption, murder, and enemies hiding in plain sight just to hold on to each other. Lightning Series, Book Two. (978-1-62639-965-5)

Summer Fling by Jean Copeland. Still jaded from a breakup years earlier, Kate struggles to trust falling in love again when a summer fling with sexy young singer Jordan rocks her off her feet. (978-1-62639-981-5)

Take Me There by Julie Cannon. Adrienne and Sloan know it would be career suicide to mix business with pleasure, however tempting it is. But what's the harm? They're both consenting adults. Who would know? (978-1-62639-917-4)

The Girl Who Wasn't Dead by Samantha Boyette. A year ago, someone tried to kill Jenny Lewis. Tonight she's ready to find out who it was. (978-1-62639-950-1)

Unchained Memories by Dena Blake. Can a woman give herself completely when she's left a piece of herself behind? (978-1-62639-993-8)

Walking Through Shadows by Sheri Lewis Wohl. All Molly wanted to do was go backpacking…in her own century (978-1-62639-968-6)

A Lamentation of Swans by Valerie Bronwen. Ariel Montgomery returns to Sea Oats to try to save her broken marriage but soon finds herself also fighting to save her own life and catch a murderer. (978-1-62639-828-3)

Freedom to Love by Ronica Black. What happens when the woman who spent her lifetime worrying about caring for her family, finally finds the freedom to love without borders? (978-1-63555-001-6)

House of Fate by Barbara Ann Wright. Two women must throw off the lives they've known as a guardian and an assassin and save two rival houses before their secrets tear the galaxy apart. (978-1-62639-780-4)

Planning for Love by Erin Dutton. Could true love be the one thing that wedding coordinator Faith McKenna didn't plan for? (978-1-62639-954-9)

Sidebar by Carsen Taite. Judge Camille Avery and her clerk, attorney West Fallon, agree on little except their mutual attraction, but can their relationship and their careers survive a headline-grabbing case? (978-1-62639-752-1)

Sweet Boy and Wild One by T. L. Hayes. When Rachel Cole meets soulful singer Bobby Layton at an open mic, she is immediately in thrall. What she soon discovers will rock her world in ways she never imagined. (978-1-62639-963-1)

To Be Determined by Mardi Alexander and Laurie Eichler. Charlie Dickerson escapes her life in the US to rescue Australian wildlife with Pip Atkins, but can they save each other? (978-1-62639-946-4)

True Colors by Yolanda Wallace. Blogger Robby Rawlins plans to use First Daughter Taylor Crenshaw to get ahead, but she never planned on falling in love with her in the process. (978-1-62639-927-3)

Unexpected by Jenny Frame. When Dale McGuire falls for Rebecca Harper, the mother of the son she never knew she had, will Rebecca's troubled past stop them from making the family they both truly crave? (978-1-62639-942-6)

Canvas for Love by Charlotte Greene. When ghosts from Amelia's past threaten to undermine their relationship, Chloé must navigate the greatest romance of her life without losing sight of who she is. (978-1-62639-944-0)

Heart Stop by Radclyffe. Two women, one with a damaged body, the other a damaged spirit, challenge each other to dare to live again. (978-1-62639-899-3)

Repercussions by Jessica L. Webb. Someone planted information in Edie Black's brain and now they want it back, but with the protection of shy former soldier Skye Kenny, Edie has a chance at life and love. (978-1-62639-925-9)

Spark by Catherine Friend. Jamie's life is turned upside down when her consciousness travels back to 1560 and lands in the body of one of Queen Elizabeth I's ladies-in-waiting…or has she totally lost her grip on reality? (978-1-62639-930-3)

Taking Sides by Kathleen Knowles. When passion and politics collide, can love survive? (978-1-62639-876-4)

Thorns of the Past by Gun Brooke. Former cop Darcy Flynn's heart broke when her career on the force ended in disgrace, but perhaps saving Sabrina Hawk's life will mend it in more ways than one. (978-1-62639-857-3)

You Make Me Tremble by Karis Walsh. Seismologist Casey Radnor comes to the San Juan Islands to study an earthquake but finds her heart shaken by passion when she meets animal rescuer Iris Mallery. (978-1-62639-901-3)

Complications by MJ Williamz. Two women battle for the heart of one. (978-1-62639-769-9)

Crossing the Wide Forever by Missouri Vaun. As Cody Walsh and Lillie Ellis face the perils of the untamed West, they discover that love's uncharted frontier isn't for the weak in spirit or the faint of heart. (978-1-62639-851-1)

Fake It Till You Make It by M. Ullrich. Lies will lead to trouble, but can they lead to love? (978-1-62639-923-5)

Girls Next Door by Sandy Lowe and Stacia Seaman eds. Best-selling romance authors tell it from the heart—sexy, romantic stories of falling for the girls next door. (978-1-62639-916-7)

Pursuit by Jackie D. The pursuit of the most dangerous terrorist in America will crack the lines of friendship and love, and not everyone will make it out under the weight of duty and service. (978-1-62639-903-7)

Shameless by Brit Ryder. Confident Emery Pearson knows exactly what she's looking for in a no-strings-attached hookup, but can a spontaneous interlude open her heart to more? (978-1-63555-006-1)

The Practitioner by Ronica Black. Sometimes love comes calling whether you're ready for it or not. (978-1-62639-948-8)

Unlikely Match by Fiona Riley. When an ambitious PR exec and her super-rich coding geek-girl client fall in love, they learn that giving something up may be the only way to have everything. (978-1-62639-891-7)

Where Love Leads by Erin McKenzie. A high school counselor and the mom of her new student bond in support of the troubled girl, never expecting deeper feelings to emerge, testing the boundaries of their relationship. (978-1-62639-991-4)